CAPTIVE FOR THE SHEIKH'S PLEASURE

BY
CAROL MARINELLI

MILLS & BOON

> MORAY COUNCIL
> LIBRARIES &
> INFO.SERVICES
>
> 20 43 55 88
>
> Askews & Holts
>
> RF

® and TM are trademarks owned and used by the trademark owner and/or its licensee. Trademarks marked with ® are registered with the United Kingdom Patent Office and/or the Office for Harmonisation in the Internal Market and in other countries.

First Published in Great Britain 2017
By Mills & Boon, an imprint of HarperCollins*Publishers*
1 London Bridge Street, London, SE1 9GF

© 2017 Carol Marinelli

ISBN: 978-0-263-92495-4

Our policy is to use papers that are natural, renewable and recyclable products and made from wood grown in sustainable forests. The logging and manufacturing processes conform to the legal environmental regulations of the country of origin.

Printed and bound in Spain
by CPI, Barcelona

Carol Marinelli recently filled in a form asking for her job title. Thrilled to be able to put down her answer, she put 'writer'. Then it asked what Carol did for relaxation and she put down the truth—'writing'. The third question asked for her hobbies. Well, not wanting to look obsessed, she crossed her fingers and answered 'swimming'—but, given that the chlorine in the pool does terrible things to her highlights, I'm sure you can guess the real answer!

Visit the Author Profile page
at millsandboon.co.uk for more titles.

CHAPTER ONE

'I WOULD NEVER have gone if you'd told me!'

Maggie Delaney was less than impressed as she made her way back to the hostel in Zayrinia with her roommate Suzanne.

Red-haired and with fair skin, Maggie had caught far too much of the Arabian sun but it wasn't that which was concerning her now—the innocent boat trip Maggie had been expecting had been far from that! 'It was practically an orgy.'

'I didn't know how it was going to turn out,' Suzanne said. 'I honestly thought that we'd be snorkelling. Oh, come on, Maggie, loosen up!'

Maggie had been told that rather too many times in her lifetime and especially over the past year.

She wasn't particularly close to Suzanne. They had met a few months ago when they had been working at the same bar and had caught up by chance here in Zayrinia.

For Maggie it was the end of a year-long working holiday and it had been the most amazing year of her life. She had travelled across Europe and Asia and had saved just enough money to go a little off the beaten path on her return journey home. She had squeezed in a stopover in Zayrinia on the last leg of her journey but, even prior to landing, Maggie had promptly fallen in love with the place.

Looking out of the window as the plane had turned in its path she had watched the desert give way to a stunning city—glittering high-rise buildings contrasted with an ancient walled citadel. And then on the final approach they had flown over the glistening ocean and the harbour lined with luxurious yachts. At her first glimpse of Zayrinia, Maggie had found herself entranced.

Today was the anniversary of her mother's death and so she had awoken feeling somewhat low. Then Suzanne had told her that she had a plus-one ticket on a boating trip out to the coral reef.

Maggie's trepidation had started even before boarding.

Instead of a snorkelling boat, they had approached a seriously luxurious yacht but Suzanne had waved away her concerns when Maggie had voiced them.

'My treat—' Suzanne had smiled '—before you head back to London. Are you looking forward to going home?'

Maggie had thought for a moment and had been just about to answer when Suzanne had cut in, 'Sorry, that was insensitive, given that you don't have anyone waiting there for you.'

Suzanne's insensitive apology had hurt more than the original comment, but Maggie simply hadn't known how to respond. She had told Suzanne ages ago that she had been in and out of foster and care homes since she was seven and didn't have any family.

'Or do you have people waiting?' Suzanne persisted. 'Do you still see any of your foster families?'

'No!'

Maggie's response was swift and a touch harsh. She was well aware that she came across as rather brusque at times. It was something she had been trying to work on during her year away. But opening up to others didn't come easily at all and Suzanne had touched on a very raw nerve. At the age of twelve, Maggie had been promised the world; for a few short months she had believed she was a part of a family. It had happened once before.

A year after her mother had died a young couple had taken her in, but their marriage had broken up and she had gone back to care. For a while she had received birthday and Christmas cards but they had petered out. It had hurt, of course, though nothing compared to what had happened a few years later when another family had taken her in. Maggie had expected nothing by then, but Diane, her foster mother, had insisted on giving Maggie the world before coldly taking it back.

It was something Maggie did her level best not to think about; she hadn't even told her best friend, Flo, what had happened that awful day.

'I have friends,' Maggie said, trying not to sound too defensive and trying not to let Suzanne hear her hurt.

'Of course you do,' Suzanne said. 'It's not the same, though, is it?'

Maggie didn't answer.

Suzanne often left her feeling rather sideswiped. Maggie was trying to be more trusting and open with people, but it didn't come easily. She was very aware that she was a touch cynical and always kept her guard up. She'd had to in some of the places she had lived.

Still, she tried.

And so, rather than explain the hurt the remark had

caused, and rather than question just where Suzanne had got the invitation from, Maggie boarded.

As the yacht set off, it became increasingly clear to Maggie that they weren't on a trip out to the coral reef. Instead, it was a very exclusive party and it would seem that they were there to pretty up the numbers!

But, other than jumping overboard, there was little she could do.

And so, wearing nothing more than a bikini and sarong, Maggie felt underdressed and over-exposed. She tried to grin and bear it at first but was all too aware of the roaming eyes drifting over her body. It made her feel supremely uncomfortable, as well as irritated, as Suzanne constantly told her to relax.

Maggie declined the free-flowing champagne that was floating around but, sick of water and needing something sweet in the fierce sun, she asked for a mocktail.

It was spicy and laced with cinnamon and tasted utterly delectable, until it was halfway down and Maggie suddenly felt dizzy and ill.

Perhaps they had got her order wrong—though Maggie doubted it—but was grateful when Suzanne steered her away from the blazing sun and led her to a cabin to lie down.

'You were gone for ages,' Suzanne said as the hostel came into sight. 'Come on, spill, what did you and the sexy prince get up to?'

Maggie halted mid-stride. 'Nothing,' she responded. 'How was I supposed to know it was the royal cabin?'

'And how was I?' Suzanne calmly answered. 'Maggie, it was an honest mistake.'

Maggie shrugged and did her best to let it go. She

seemed to have to do that an awful lot around Suzanne, though. But again she said nothing, telling herself that it really had been a simple mix-up and thankfully no harm had been done. In fact, it had been nice to hide for a couple of hours in the cool of the cabin, though it had been a touch awkward at first when the prince had come in to find her lying on his bed!

Suzanne assumed more had happened.

It hadn't.

Nothing like that ever did!

Maggie sometimes wondered if she had been born missing a fuse, for not even the sight of a sexy prince with just a towel around his hips could ignite her.

It had been a touch awkward at first; she'd apologised, of course, and they'd ended up talking.

There had been nothing more to it than that.

As they walked into the hostel, all Maggie wanted was to have a shower, some supper and answer a few emails. Paul, her boss at the café where she had worked before heading off on her trip, was short staffed and had asked her to let him know when she would be home and whether she wanted her old job back.

She also wanted to send a long email to her friend Flo who would, no doubt, laugh her head off at the thought of Maggie alone in a bedroom with a sexy prince and nothing other than conversation taking place!

After that she just wanted to read in peace.

Perhaps peace was a slightly tall order given that she was in a four-bed dorm at the hostel, but Suzanne was doing the star-gazing tour tonight and the two other women had checked out this morning.

Hopefully nobody else had checked in!

'Maggie!'

She heard her name being called from Reception and Maggie headed over to the desk as Suzanne made her way to the dorm.

Tazia, the receptionist, gave Maggie an apologetic smile as she approached. 'We have just heard that tomorrow's star-gazing trip has had to be cancelled as there is a simoom predicted.'

'Simoom?'

'A large sandstorm. I've got a refund here for you.'

'Oh, no.' Maggie sighed because she had been really looking forward to it.

'I am sorry,' Tazia said as she handed over the cash. 'The earliest I can book is Monday but even that would depend on the storm clearing in time.'

Maggie shook her head. Her flight was on Monday morning, so that was no good. 'How about tonight?' Maggie asked, even though she was incredibly tired.

'It's fully booked. I tried a couple of other operators but given the unpredictability of the weather most aren't taking any tourists out tonight.'

It was such a disappointment and Maggie could have kicked herself for not booking the trip for tonight when she'd had a chance. Though she knew the real reason why she'd avoided this evening's excursion—Suzanne had booked a ticket and, in truth, Maggie had wanted to take this trip alone.

'Thanks anyway,' Maggie said. 'If there are any cancellations, can you let me know?'

'I wouldn't count on it.' Tazia shook her head. 'You are tenth on the list.'

It simply wasn't meant to be.

Maggie went into the dorm to collect her toiletry bag before heading for the shower.

'What did Tazia want?' Suzanne asked.

'The trip to the desert tomorrow has been cancelled.' Maggie sighed. 'I'm going to take a shower.'

'While you do, is it okay if I borrow your phone? I just want to send a text to Glen.'

Suzanne's phone had got wet and so for the last few days she had been using Maggie's.

'Sure,' Maggie agreed.

The shower was far from luxurious but after a year spent in hostels Maggie was more than used to it.

The water was cool and refreshing and so Maggie stayed under for a while, rinsing off the copious amounts of sun lotion she had applied to her pale skin. Then she massaged conditioner into her long red curls while trying to let go of the hurt that Suzanne's thoughtless words had caused.

'It's not the same, though, is it?'

It had been a throwaway comment, yet it still buzzed around in her head and so, rather than think of old hurts, Maggie turned her mind to all that had happened today.

Or rather all that hadn't!

She was terribly aware that she was light years behind her peers in the sexual department.

It wasn't through lack of opportunity. In the café where she worked at home there were endless clients who tried to flirt or outright asked her out. Occasionally Maggie went along, but it was always the same outcome—a few awkward kisses were the sum total of her dating repertoire.

Still, even if there hadn't been so much as a flicker of attraction, Hazin had been interesting to talk to. For all his good looks and privilege, he had seemed refreshingly down to earth. Usually when she told anyone that she had no family they would offer awkward sympathy. Hazin had grinned and told her she was the lucky one, then had proceeded to tell her about his parents and the cold way in which he and his older brother, Ilyas, had been raised.

'Are you close to your brother?' Maggie had asked.

'Who? Ilyas?' Hazin grinned. 'No one could get close to him.'

Yes, it had been interesting indeed, and now Maggie could not wait to email Flo and bring her up to date. She turned off the taps and reached around the curtain for her towel and change of clothes.

For Maggie there was no question of drying off in the open dressing area. She had lived in too many places and with too many strangers to trust others and so always emerged from the shower fully dressed.

Thankfully, the copious amounts of sun lotion she had applied through the day seemed to have done the trick because as she dried off it would seem only her shoulders were a touch pink. The rest of her was as white and freckled as ever.

Maggie was incapable of getting a tan and had long since given up trying. In fact, she looked as if she'd come from an English winter rather than a sun-soaked Middle Eastern summer.

She pulled on some pale yoga pants and a long-sleeved top; though the days were hot, the desert nights were cold. Maggie was just thinking about what to have for supper when she returned to the dorm and saw that Suzanne was packing.

'Getting ready for tonight?' Maggie asked.

'No,' Suzanne said. 'There's been a bit of a change

of plan. I'm checking out and meeting up with Glen in Dubai.'

'Oh,' Maggie said. 'Tonight?'

'I'm to collect the ticket at the airport.'

'Wow! Well, I guess this is goodbye, then.'

Suzanne nodded and smiled. 'It's been nice spending time with you.'

'It has,' Maggie said politely. There was no offer to keep in touch, from either of them.

Maggie didn't find goodbyes hard in the least—her childhood had guaranteed that she was very used to them.

To this day, she could still recall coming home from her *new* school and racing through the door of her *new* home to see her *new* puppy, only to be greeted by her social worker and told it was time to return to ways of old.

Maggie could never forget Diane's cold blue eyes flick away when Maggie had asked to see the puppy.

'Can I say goodbye to Patch?' she had asked.

'Patch isn't here,' the social worker had said.

He must have been too much trouble too.

Maggie hadn't cried as her bags had been loaded into the social worker's car and she certainly hadn't cried when she'd walked out of that house.

Even back in a *new* care home she had not cried that night in bed.

Tears didn't help. If they did, her mother would still be alive.

Yes, she was very used to goodbyes and, in truth, this particular one with Suzanne came as a bit of a relief. Maggie was happy with her own company and she found Suzanne a bit pushy.

'Hey,' Suzanne suddenly said, and opened up her travel wallet. 'You could use this.'

Maggie looked down at the coveted ticket for the star-gazing trip tonight and a smile lit her face. 'Are you sure?'

'Well, I shan't be using it. I was going to hand it back in at the desk and get a refund…'

'Don't!' Maggie yelped, and handed over the cash that Tazia had just given her. 'I'm way down the cancellation list.'

'You'll have to use my name, then. I booked the Star Package, with a camel ride included.' She gave Maggie a smile. 'You'd better get a move on, the bus leaves at eight.'

There was just time for Maggie to tie back her hair and pack a small overnight bag as Suzanne pulled on her backpack.

'Well, I'm off,' Suzanne said.

'Safe travels.'

'You too! And don't forget,' Suzanne said as she headed out of the door, 'for tonight you're Suzanne.'

CHAPTER TWO

CROWN PRINCE SHEIKH ILYAS OF ZAYRINIA had been born to be king.

And that was all.

His parents had had no real desire to be parents, neither had they taken delight in their baby.

They'd delivered for their country the necessary heir and then moved on to produce the spare.

Ilyas had barely seen them, unless for official duties, and had been raised in a distant area of the stunning, sprawling palace. He'd been fed and groomed by royal nannies and immersed in the teachings by elders.

It had been a busy little life and one utterly devoid of affection.

When Ilyas was four, Prince Hazin of Zayrinia had been born, thus pushing the uncle his father loathed down to third in the line of succession. Only when, two months later, Ilyas had stood on the royal balcony beside his parents had he come to realise that the tiny infant his mother held in her arms was, in fact, his brother. He'd kept craning his head to have a peek but had been sternly told to look ahead.

'Can I see him?' Ilyas had asked his mother, the

queen, as they'd moved from the balcony and back into the palace.

But his mother had shaken her head. 'Hazin has to go to the nursery,' she'd informed Ilyas as she'd handed over her baby to the wet nurse for feeding. 'And you have your afternoon lessons to attend, although King Ahmed wishes to speak with you first.'

Ilyas had known, from the use of his father's title, that it would not be a fatherly chat.

It never was.

He'd been led to his father, who had been speaking with Mahmoud, his vizier.

'Well done, Your Highness,' Mahmoud had said, for it had been a very large crowd that had gathered outside the palace to greet the new prince. The king, though, had been less than impressed with Ilyas's behaviour out on the balcony.

'Don't fidget so much in future,' his father had told him.

'I just wanted to see what my brother looks like.'

'He's just a baby.' The king had shrugged. 'Now, remember, in future always look ahead no matter what else goes on around you.'

For the most part, the brothers had been segregated. Ilyas had been considered too far ahead in his studies to be held back. Hazin, who was nothing more than a substitute, had eventually been schooled overseas in England.

It was Ilyas who had been born to be king.

For his first two decades he had absorbed the teachings and wisdom from his elders and everyone had assumed that Ilyas agreed with them, for he performed all his duties well.

His parents believed that the strict discipline of his upbringing had worked well, but this was not filial obedience. What they failed to understand was that it was Ilyas himself who was disciplined—he had *chosen* to abide by their rules.

For now.

When Ilyas had turned twenty-two, tragedy had struck the palace. His father and adviser had decided that a royal wedding would raise the spirits of the country and that it was time for Ilyas to marry. They had called a meeting to inform him of their decision.

But Ilyas had shaken his head.

'It is not necessary for me to marry yet.'

King Ahmed had frowned at his son's response, assuming that Ilyas had misunderstood him, for the king had been used to his demands being met.

But Ilyas had held firm on the subject of marriage.

Ilyas had indeed taken his father's advice to look ahead. He'd had plans for the future, many of them, in fact, but there was no one he could risk sharing those plans with.

No one.

Marriage was not something he'd wanted to consider, at least for a couple of decades, and so again he'd declined his father's suggestion. The king had grown more insistent.

'A wedding, followed by an heir, would be pleasing for our people,' he'd told his elder son, assuming that was that and they could move on to the next matter, but Ilyas would not be swayed.

'The people need to grieve in their own time,' Ilyas had said. 'I shall marry when the time is right, not when you decide.' He'd glanced over at Mahmoud, whose face had paled as Ilyas had delivered this challenge to the absolute authority of the king.

'I said that I would like you to marry,' the king had bellowed, the command inherent in his tone.

'Marriage is a lifetime commitment and one I am not yet willing to make. For now, the harem shall suffice.' He'd looked over at Mahmoud again and moved on the meeting. 'Next item.'

Ilyas was stern yet fair, level rather than cold, and the people of Zayrinia adored him and silently longed for the day he was king.

As the king's health had declined, Ilyas's power had subtly risen, though not enough for his liking. But on this particular Friday, as Mahmoud stated that a fresh crisis threatened the palace, it was Ilyas who took control.

'It is already being dealt with,' Ilyas informed his father calmly, though the amber in his hazel eyes flashed with irritation. Why the hell had Mahmoud raised his younger brother's latest indiscretions in front of the king?

'But what sort of party was it?' the king asked.

'It was just a gathering,' Ilyas smoothly answered. 'You yourself said that you wanted Hazin to come home more often.'

'Yes, but to attend to royal duties,' the king said, and then looked at his aide and asked again, 'What sort of party was held on his yacht?'

Ilyas could very well guess the type of debauched gathering that had taken place.

His brother was famous for them.

Almost.

The palace had their work cut out concealing the scandals that Hazin left in his wake and the king had recently decided that enough was enough. King Ahmed al-Razim was more than prepared to disinherit his youngest and strip him of privilege and title.

Most would say Hazin deserved it.

Ilyas was not swayed by others, though.

Not even by his father, the king.

'I discussed it with Hazin before he left,' Ilyas informed his father. 'He assured me that it was just a day out with friends before he headed back to London.'

'And did you remind him that if there is one more whisper of scandal the London apartment will be off limits to him?' King Ahmed checked. 'Did you tell him that his accounts shall be severed and there shall be no more access to the royal jets and yachts?'

'Yes, I told him,' Ilyas responded.

'Perhaps if he has to work for a living he might spend his money more wisely.'

'Hazin is wealthy in his own right,' Ilyas reminded his father.

'Few could be wealthy enough to support his habits,' the king hissed. 'It had better be dealt with, Ilyas.' He strode out of the office and, once the doors parted and closed behind him, a worried Mahmoud spoke.

'Your father needs to know that the palace is being blackmailed in order to keep Hazin's secrets. If this gets out it will be a disaster,' Mahmoud insisted. 'Hazin has been given enough rope—there have been too many last chances.'

'I said that I shall deal with it,' Ilyas warned.

'King Ahmed needs to know! These people need to

be paid off. I have been his senior advisor for almost half a century—'

'It must be almost time for retirement, then,' Ilyas cut in, and he watched as Mahmoud puffed in indignation. 'The palace must not give in to threats.' He gave a dismissive shrug. 'I don't believe there even is a sex tape.'

'I am not so sure,' Mahmoud said and, now that the king was gone, he admitted to more. 'Unless the payment is made by midday on Monday they will release the footage. The woman has made contact again.'

Ilyas read through the messages that had been coming through to the private server for the past week, but the demands were more specific now—stating the sum of money required and where and when it was to be deposited to prevent the release of the tape.

'She is bold,' Mahmoud said.

Ilyas did not agree with the advisor's findings.

'No,' he said, again reading the message. 'If this Suzanne believes that she can bribe me she is a fool.'

He examined the attached photos and knew at first glance that they had been taken aboard his brother's yacht.

A stunning redhead with green eyes and delicate-looking pale skin had been photographed in a willow-green bikini.

There was another photo, grainy as if it had been taken from afar and zoomed in, that showed her lying on a bed as Hazin walked into what Ilyas knew to be the royal cabin.

The message warned that the more explicit footage taken inside the cabin would be shocking, but Ilyas wasn't buying it.

'If they had more they would already have sent it.'

'They have more,' Mahmoud said as Ilyas moved to the next photo.

It was a full frontal of his younger brother in a less than regal pose.

Hazin was completely naked, though, in fairness, Ilyas could see he was just rinsing off, presumably after a swim.

'This is nothing that our long-suffering public has not already seen. There are more full-frontal naked pictures of Hazin circulating on the Internet than I care to count. It's nothing.'

Well, hardly nothing—Hazin took after his brother in that department and this particular image made no secret of that fact.

There was another issue, though.

'This was taken in Zayrinian waters.' Mahmoud pointed out exactly what Ilyas was thinking. 'You can even see the palace in the distance. The king promised his people that there would be no more scandal from Hazin.'

It was his father who was the fool, then.

Hazin and Ilyas might be similar in *certain* departments but were completely different in nature. Ilyas simply didn't deal in emotion and so rarely encountered it that, if he did, it held little sway on his decisions. He was always focused and supremely composed while his brother, on the other hand, ran wild. Hazin was a loose cannon who chose to live the life of a playboy, yet, Ilyas was certain, after the warning he had served his brother prior to his visit, he would not have brought this behaviour home on this occasion.

Right now, Hazin was aboard the royal jet and heading back to London, oblivious to the latest development in the unfolding scandal.

'Sit tight,' Ilyas told Mahmoud. 'If there is any further contact I am to be informed. Not my father,' he added.

He could see Mahmoud's silent struggle as to whether or not he should brief the king.

Over and over Ilyas had warned Hazin to be mindful of long-range lenses but these images looked like they had been taken from a phone.

Probably not a professional, then.

But, no, he would not be swayed.

Ilyas again flicked through the photos. Despite his blasé response to Mahmoud, the naked image alone could prove extremely damaging. The people more easily dismissed Hazin's transgressions while overseas, but, Ilyas knew, they would not be so forgiving if Hazin brought scandal home.

Then he looked at the woman, uncertain if she was this Suzanne woman or just the lure used to tempt Hazin.

He could actually see how his brother might have been taken in.

She was stunning.

Her long, wavy red hair was swept back by the wind and her body was not the manufactured kind that so often attended parties such as this.

She was incredibly pale with a dusting of freckles on her arms and thighs. Her body was slender and her curves subtle and very feminine, while in the picture her lips were full and parted in a smile.

Yet it did not reach her eyes and Ilyas was certain the smile she wore was a false one.

Yes, she was the smiling assassin indeed.

'Do nothing without my instruction,' Ilyas reiterated. 'And contact me if necessary.

'I am going to the *hammam*.'

'Your Highness.' Mahmoud nodded and bowed as Ilyas departed.

The palace was beyond exquisite.

The huge, sprawling, ivory marble construction appeared, from an external vantage, to be set on a long red canyon on the edge of the Persian Gulf. It looked down on the bustling city while the westerly wing overlooked the endless desert.

The palace was a true masterpiece and had been built around a natural oasis that existed to this day. It was vast and contained within it many residences, as well as formal function areas and spaces for worship.

It held more secrets, though, for it was not just set on the cliff—it had actually been carved from within.

The tunnels beneath were all lined with ancient drawings and detailed mosaics. Ilyas descended first the carved marble steps, which soon gave way to steps carved into the bedrock.

Here the air was cooler. Ilyas walked through his private tunnel, the path lit by huge pillar candles. With the sound of cascading water in the distance he hoped the gnawing of concern in his gut would soon melt away.

The *hammam* was divine, and certain areas were accessible from several routes but few were allowed to venture where Ilyas did now.

It was a world few knew existed.

A natural cave waterfall was the centrepiece and the constant torrent provided a stunning audio-visual backdrop. There were several pools and smaller waterfalls that ran into larger cave pools beneath the *hammam*. When the light struck right, the entrance to one of the cave pools glowed a deep red from un-mined rubies. By day, occasional shafts of sunlight beamed in and created a natural cathedral; by night it was the stars and moon that showered the waters with their light. It was a royal retreat indeed.

Ilyas stripped out of his robe and dropped into a deep plunge pool, fully immersing himself. But as he rose to the surface his tension refused to relent.

Despite his calm reaction in front of Mahmoud, Ilyas was deeply concerned.

Ilyas knew he appeared as cold and indifferent as his father but he had not been chipped from the same block of ice.

He did not want Hazin to be disinherited, yet he knew that day was approaching. Despite his best efforts, nothing seemed to be able to divert the train wreck in motion.

There was nothing he could do except remain vigilant, but for now Ilyas did his best to relax.

Rarely did he have an entire weekend to do with as he pleased.

Usually there were several engagements to attend and often he travelled overseas, both forging new relationships and attempting to repair the disastrous ones his father's rule had created.

Summoning one of the masseuses, Ilyas walked over to the large marble stone at the centre of the area and lay on his stomach as his skin was rubbed with salt.

Soon he would get up and rinse off under the waterfall. He looked out to the desert from his privileged vantage point—few even knew it existed, for there was an uninterrupted view of desert sands and sky.

Later he would make his selection from the harem.

His father still regularly pushed him to select a bride but Ilyas consistently refused.

And who could blame him!

Along one of the tunnels he could hear the distant sounds of laughter from the harem and there was a velvet rope above him that at any moment he could pull. As he lay there, with his head on his forearm and sex on his mind, Ilyas thought of the woman in the photo that Mahmoud had handed him earlier.

Deft hands were working the small of his back but it was not the skill of the masseuse that had Ilyas shift his position on the cold marble stone.

It was the thought of the woman and her blaze of red hair and pale freckled skin that had him hardening.

'Your Highness.' The sound of Mahmoud's voice was not in the least welcome. 'I apologise for disturbing you.'

Unless Hazin's plane had crashed or his father had passed, Mahmoud had no business disturbing Ilyas in the *hammam*. 'What now?' he asked angrily.

'The woman in the photo, the one...'

'What about her?' Ilyas snapped. He certainly did not need a refresher course on the woman to whom Mahmoud referred, for she was currently on more than his mind.

'I have just found out that she is still in the country. Apparently she is booked on a tour tonight.'

'Then you were right the first time,' Ilyas growled. 'She is a fool.' For no one with any sense would remain in the country having served such an explicit threat.

'We have traced her phone and it would seem that she is attending the star-gazing trip.'

'There shall be few stars tonight since there is a simoom expected.' It was not due here until tomorrow but the red of the sky was foreboding. 'There should be no tourists out in the desert tonight.'

'The tour went ahead. She is out there, Your Highness,' Mahmoud said, and gestured to the desert.

Ilyas knew that some of the tour operators ignored warnings. It was an ongoing issue but not one that concerned him now.

'I am sure she is calling our bluff but we have a team investigating.' Ilyas dismissed him but then he wavered. His father had made it exceptionally clear that Hazin was on his final warning.

If there was the slightest truth behind this threat, the results for Hazin would be dire indeed.

'Bring this Suzanne to me.'

'Here?' Mahmoud was aghast. 'If the king gets wind—'

'Not here,' Ilyas interrupted. 'Have her taken to the desert abode. I shall speak with her there.'

'You could well find yourself stranded.'

Ilyas was more than used to the tricks of the desert and always enjoyed his time there. He drew on it for strength and wisdom, and the thought of being stranded didn't trouble him in the least.

'Perhaps this Suzanne should have considered that before firing off her threats.'

Ilyas flicked his hand to tell Mahmoud to get to work and carry out his orders and then he went to reach for the rope above to select his concubine. His hand halted midway as he changed his mind and instead rose from the table and walked over to the running water, where he rinsed off.

He would deal with this impossible woman first, and *then* he would select from the harem.

CHAPTER THREE

MAGGIE DIDN'T WANT to admit it.

Even to herself.

But, after all the effort to get here, the much-awaited star-gazing trip wasn't all she had hoped it would be.

Unlike everything else she had experienced here in Zayrinia, the trip to the desert had proved more than a little touristy.

In truth, the journey *deep into the desert* had taken less than an hour and that allowed for all the time it had taken to mount and dismount from their camels.

'At the wishes of the Bedouins,' one of the guides explained, 'we are forbidden from going any further.'

A couple complained rather loudly but the guide explained that there was nothing that could be done.

Yet.

'We have put in several formal requests for the law to be changed,' he said. 'The final decision rests with the king.'

Having lined up and been served dinner, the group had sat on rugs by a huge fire and watched belly dancers as the sun had started to set.

But as the sun dimmed, so too did the hopes of a night of stargazing. The sky was overcast and the visibility was low due to the gathering sandstorm in the east.

It was still rather spectacular, though.

The sand and dust carried by the wind turned the tiny new moon pale crimson and Maggie watched, awe-struck, as it drifted behind and then peeked out of the huge rolling clouds.

The tales around the campfire were interesting too, and the guide used his hands as he told expressive tales.

'Beneath the palace there is a river where, to this day, the water runs red. It marks the spot where a young prince was denied marriage to his lover and died of a broken heart.' Maggie was wide-eyed.

'Since then,' the guide told them, 'the crown prince does not court. Love is for lesser mortals. A king must think only with his head.'

'Does the water really run red?' asked a woman to the side of Maggie, but the guide had moved on to another tale.

'The palace is built on the ruins of what once was a harem,' he explained. 'The concubines feasted and rested until summoned by a bell. There were many wild and decadent times but it was considered far safer than allowing a virile prince loose in the land with his heart. It is said that the winds that are heard at night are, in fact, the sounds of debauchery carrying across time…'

And the winds were starting to gather.

The campfire tales were halted and the guides gathered in a confab. Maggie guessed they were deciding if the trip should simply be cancelled. But then the annoying couple loudly pointed out that in the event of adverse weather conditions a full refund would be given.

The tour would go ahead!

People were soon being guided to their designated sleeping areas but Maggie continued to stand by the fire. Beyond it was a huge canyon and atop that the outline of the palace. She thought of days long gone and the stories of long-dead royals who were given everything except for love.

Even without stars, Zayrinia, Maggie decided, was beautiful beyond words.

'Suzanne!'

Maggie only turned when the name was called for a third time and only because of the impatient tone, but then she realised the summons was aimed at her.

Ah, yes, for tonight, she was Suzanne.

The organiser waved her over and gestured to the area that would be Maggie's home until sunrise.

It was a small, tented area, with a simple mattress where she could either lie and continue to view the night sky or, as was strongly suggested, she could pull the canopy over.

Maggie nodded and thanked him. Refusing to give in just yet, she kept the canopy open, and kicking off her shoes bedded down for what remained of the night.

There appeared not a single star in the sky.

To her left, the couple who had argued about everything were now complaining about the hard mattress and there was a man snoring to her right.

Of all the many highlights of her year, Zayrinia had become her favourite. She had instantly felt somehow drawn to the land.

That in itself was rare for Maggie.

She had learnt not to get attached to people, let alone locations, yet there was something about Zayrinia that entranced her.

It really did, Maggie thought as she gazed up at the dark, heavy sky.

While there wasn't a star to be seen, the clouds billowed and raced so swiftly it was as if the sky had been placed on fast forward, and soon the sounds of her fellow tourists were drowned out by the cries of the wind whistling through distant canyons.

It really had been the most amazing year. One that Maggie would never have embarked on had it not been for her mother.

It wasn't the lack of stars that had tears pool in her eyes, or the knowledge that her trip was drawing to a close.

The threat of tears was reserved for the very reason she was here.

Maggie missed her mother so much.

Erin Delaney had fallen pregnant when she was just seventeen and Maggie had never known her father.

Even though she had been a single, teenage mum, Erin had given her daughter a very happy childhood.

Still now, when Maggie felt alone or scared, thoughts of innocent, happy times would come to mind.

Maggie lay there remembering a time they had come from the baker's and had got caught in the rain. They had ducked under the awnings of a shop that had, though Maggie hadn't really understood then, been a travel agent.

'You need to see the world, Maggie,' her mother had said as they'd looked at a huge map in the window.

'I like it here.'

'I know you do, but there's a whole world outside London. I was going to go travelling and see it for myself...'

'But you had me instead.'

'You're the best mistake I ever made!' Erin smiled. 'But seriously, Maggie, you make sure you see the world. I'm saving up hard and next year we're going to Paris.'

They hadn't got there, though.

After a short, hard-fought battle with cancer, Erin had passed away. She'd had little money but she had left a small sum for Maggie to inherit when she turned twenty-one and it had been accompanied by a letter. In it Erin had told her daughter that she had been and still was deeply loved. Erin had said that she hoped Maggie would consider spreading her wings and taking in this wonderful world in a way that she had not.

The money had been enough to cover the airfare, but it had taken Maggie two years to save up enough to take the trip.

She had taken the train first to Paris and from there Maggie had travelled through Europe before heading to America and then Asia and Australia and home via the Middle East.

And now on the final leg of her journey, Zayrinia had won her heart.

On Monday she would be on her way back to London and a week after that she would be back working at the café.

Maggie fought to keep her eyes open, for she wanted to savour every last moment. But the day had started early and an awful lot of it had been spent in the sun. Maggie's eyes were soon closing.

At first she thought the rustle of the tent was just the wind but then Maggie felt a hand on her shoulder. For a brief second she thought it must be the guide telling her to wake up, but then the hand gripped her tighter, roughly, and even before Maggie thought to scream, she felt a hand clamp over her mouth.

It all happened so quickly—one moment Maggie was sleeping, the next she was being dragged under the canvas and through the sand.

She fought and kicked but there was more than one person and the wind was her enemy now, for it drowned the sounds of the struggle she made. She smelt body odour and felt the rough fabric of their clothes against her cheeks. But their grip on her arms and thighs only tightened as she twisted to free herself.

All to no avail.

It took less than a minute to be bundled into a vehicle and Maggie fought each second of it even as she was driven away.

'What do you want?' she asked as the hand was removed from her mouth, but there was no answer.

The vehicle came to a halt and she was dragged out. Maggie thought she had already tasted fear, but that was nothing compared to how the sand stung as it whipped at her cheeks and the wind took her breath away as she cried out at the lights from a helicopter.

'*Yalla! Yalla!*' a man urged loudly, and Maggie knew they were being told to hurry.

'Please…' she begged, not just because she was being kidnapped, but because surely it was way too windy to fly. Nothing she said or did made a difference; Maggie knew she was outnumbered and knew somehow that it was better to save her energy than to fight.

And still she refused to cry.

Careful what you wish for!

Just a few hours ago, Maggie had silently bemoaned the fact she was not deeper in the desert, and now she watched as it spread like a never-ending ocean beneath them.

It was not the first time Maggie had been wrenched from her bed.

Memories were stirring and she tried to stuff them down, but as they grew stronger she gave in, for there was strange comfort to be had in remembering those days.

As she looked through childhood memories with adult eyes, she found she could make sense of things. Time had given her perspective; what had happened to her made far more sense now than it ever had when she had been living through it.

The memories came thick and fast now. The drenching light and her bedroom full of strangers had, in fact, been the first responders when her mother had taken a serious turn for the worse.

Erin had called for an ambulance and, Maggie realised now, she must have told them she had a child sleeping in the flat.

It had felt like an invasion at the time—being lifted from her bed and carried to an ambulance.

She had held her mother's hand throughout the journey and told her she loved her over and over. At the hospital she had been led to a small room to wait and it had been there she had been told that her mother was dead.

That was fear, Maggie told herself as she stared out into the dark night.

She could deal with this.

And there had to be a logical explanation.

She remembered being driven through the night some time after her mother had died.

Again, she had been awoken, seemingly in the middle of the night.

Now, though, she recalled arriving at yet another new temporary accommodation. A couple had been eating their dinner. It had been the middle of winter and dark, but perhaps not the middle of the night as she had thought then.

There had been a more logical explanation then and there *had* to be one now.

Maggie simply could not fathom what it was.

'What do you want from me?' she asked one of the men, but either he did not understand or simply chose not to answer.

The helicopter was circling and she could feel them hover and then be lifted by a gust of wind. She could see the tension on the features of the men as the pilot fought to land them in the storm.

There was a complex beneath, the white of a large tent with a collection of smaller ones dotted around the main one, like surf on the ocean. And the sand moved in waves beneath them, not unlike the sea itself. Finally they landed and Maggie breathed a sigh of relief.

She was hauled from the helicopter and a large hand pushed her head down as she was dragged through the sands.

The air was cold, the sand stung her cheeks, and then she was pushed, or did she simply stumble?

Maggie pulled herself up to her knees, anticipating being hauled back to her feet and determined to do it herself.

It took a moment to fathom she was now alone.

The sound of the chopper combined with the shrieking wind was deafening and she put her hands over her ears, battling with too many thoughts and sensations to attempt to think clearly.

The flashing lights were lifting, the helicopter was taking off again, and Maggie covered her eyes as she realised she had been left there alone in the shifting sand.

The sharp grains blasted her cheeks and stung her eyes as she tried to gauge her surroundings. Squinting, she could just make out the white of a tent in the distance.

It was huge.

Bigger than the circus tent she had been to as a child.

And in the midst of terror, as so often happened, a happier memory flashed to mind—sitting with her mother, eating a sticky treat, laughing and laughing...

She hadn't known then just how precious that time was; it had seemed so natural to be content then. Now, though, she was a fighter and, if Maggie wanted to survive, then there was little choice but to make her way to the tent for protection.

Or perhaps not?

Briefly she turned from the tent and considered simply walking away and forcing them to come and get her.

Whoever they were.

Two steps into her journey away from the tent she gave up on the idea. There was no way she could last out here on her own.

The winds shrieked around her as Maggie reluctantly headed towards the tent, for it was like walking through molasses.

She reached the entrance and pulled a heavy drape aside, dreading what she might find—more henchmen?

More captives? Her imagination was working overtime, but not for a second had she considered that she might step into luxurious beauty.

The inside of the tent was softly lit and the sound of screeching winds was mercifully muted as the drape closed behind her. She caught strains of music and the scent of incense, and felt an irresistible pull to follow the length of the corridor ahead.

Thick carpet had replaced the sand and was soft on her bare feet; the walls were lined with a stream of tiny bells that made a soft tinkling sound as she ran her hands along them.

No one came to find her.

She walked further and came to an entrance covered by a veil of sheer fabric and she thought she must be at the centre.

Still, nothing made sense, for she had never seen such beauty before in her life. The floor was spread with rugs and was scattered with cushions. Gorgeous tapestries hung on the walls and light from many lamps danced along them. In the centre was an enclosed fire with a flue that led to the high roof of the tent. The only indication of the stark weather conditions outside was the gentle billowing of the roof as she looked up.

Maggie walked over to a low table that was laden with fruits and delicacies. There were ornate jugs that were filled to the brim and beside them were jewelled goblets, but though thirsty she did not take her fill.

'Help yourself.'

A deep voice jolted her. Maggie did not move and neither did she look around. The voice was so rich that it seemed to come from all sides and she was not certain of its direction.

'No, thank you,' Maggie said, and was both surprised and pleased that her voice did not waver.

'Turn around,' he told her. 'Or do you not have the courage to repeat your demands to my face?'

'Demands?' Now she spun and immediately wished she hadn't, for Maggie had been braced to face a monster. Instead, what she saw was a man more beautiful than any she had ever seen.

And Maggie did not want him to be.

Absolutely she did not want that to be her first thought as she faced her captor.

And she knew that this man was her captor.

Not the henchmen who had dragged her sleeping from her bed and brought her here; she knew now that they had followed his orders.

Maggie was certain that he gave orders, for it was crystal clear to her that he was a leader.

He was taller than most and wore dark layered robes; on his head was a black *kafeyah* tied with a braided rope. His clothes were immaculate, as if not so much as a grain of sand would dare to sully him.

Though unshaven, he was far from dishevelled; in fact, he was impeccably groomed. His face was chiselled, and though his eyes were an intense hazel, it was his mouth that drew her eyes.

'I assume you know why you are here?' he said and his English surprised her—or rather the clipped, well-schooled accent did.

She looked from his mouth to his eyes that flashed irritation at her lack of response, but she stared back without blinking.

Maggie refused to show fear.

And she refused to answer him.

She would say nothing until it was clear why she was here, Maggie had decided.

'Did you really think that there would be no repercussions, Suzanne?'

And then she reversed her decision not to speak.

Of course it might be far safer to say nothing, but there was one thing this man just had to understand because Maggie was finally starting to—it really was all a mix-up. Perhaps a less than simple mistake, but a mistake nonetheless. Here was the rational explanation she had been searching for earlier.

And once he knew that, she would be free.

So she cleared her throat and stated her case.

'I'm not Suzanne.'

CHAPTER FOUR

HER REVELATION DID not send him scurrying to apologise, although Maggie doubted that this man had ever scurried or apologised to anyone in his life, though she stated her case again. 'There's been a mix-up. You see, I'm not Suzanne.'

'Of course you're not.' He gave a dismissive shrug. 'I hardly expected you to use your real name.'

'But I know who she is...' Maggie was starting to see how it had happened. Oh, she had no idea what Suzanne was up to and what he might want with her, but she could now see what had occurred tonight. 'I used Suzanne's ticket to go on the desert tour. It was a last-minute change of plan.'

'So where is she now?'

'I'm not sure.' Maggie chose to be evasive, rather than reveal that Suzanne had left earlier for Dubai. 'But whatever she's involved in has nothing to do with me.'

'It has *everything* to do with you!'

'I'm not Suzanne,' she said again. 'My name is Maggie. Maggie Delaney. I don't even know who you are.'

That seemed to amuse him.

His mouth spread into a smile and he walked over to her.

Right over.

He came into her space, and as his hand moved towards her she flinched; he gripped her chin and forced her face up.

She refused to meet his eyes as he spoke.

'Allow me to introduce myself. I am Sheikh Ilyas al-Razim…'

She knew that name and her eyes met his then and all trace of that smile was gone. Contempt blazed in his eyes and his fingers were firm on her jaw as he spoke on. 'You shall deal with me now, rather than an aide. I have decided to cut the snake off at the head myself.'

'I don't know what you want with me.'

He released her then and went over to a low dark table where he retrieved a folder, which he held out to her.

'Did you enjoy your day on the royal yacht?' he asked.

With shaking hands Maggie took the folder and opened it. A photo of her wearing just a bikini was the first thing she saw.

In it she was smiling, but Maggie could well remember the awkwardness of that moment and could see the grit of her teeth. It paled in comparison to her discomfort now as she realised she had been photographed and that he must have examined it.

'There are more,' he told her.

And there were, for there she was lying on a bed as Hazin came into the cabin.

Maggie felt sick.

'Keep going,' he said calmly.

The next was an image of the royal prince whose cabin she had inadvertently ended up in. Hazin was laughing and naked! Very quickly she jerked her eyes away, but there was no solace for her gaze went straight to Ilyas's.

And his eyes were not kind.

'What is your relationship with my brother?' he asked.

Oh, this was the older brother Hazin had spoken less than fondly of.

'Answer the question. What is your relationship with my brother?'

'I don't have one.'

'So you often share a bed with men you have no relationship with?'

'Not often, no…'

He didn't get her nervous humour—the vague joke that had shot out, because Maggie had never shared a bed with a man in her life.

'When these sex tapes surface…'

She laughed.

Possibly it was the shock of being stranded in the desert that made it such a nervous laugh. Or perhaps it was the irony that she, a twenty-four-year-old virgin, was being accused of taking part in some salacious scandal with a royal prince.

'You find this funny?' he checked.

'A little,' Maggie said. 'Well, I find it bizarre—although possibly it's a nervous reaction—but, yes, the thought of me appearing in a sex tape is laughable.'

He frowned and Maggie guessed this foreboding man had no idea what being nervous felt like, and neither would he laugh easily. She spoke on, eager to clear up the mistake. 'I can assure you there are no sex tapes—at least, none with me in them.'

He said nothing.

'I had sunstroke,' Maggie explained. 'I just went to lie down.'

'You've recovered quickly,' he mused. 'Given that you were well enough to go on your little tour.' He seemed to tire of her then. 'We will speak later.' He called out in Arabic and there was the sound of small bells and two women dressed in black came in. 'Go and make yourself presentable.'

'Presentable?' Her voice was incredulous, but then nerves flooded in as she was terribly aware he had seen photos of her with very little on and perhaps that was his reason for bringing her here. 'If you think for one moment—'

'Go and clean up,' Ilyas interrupted.

'The only thing that needs cleaning up is your mistake,' Maggie said. 'You can't keep me here. I'm due to fly home on Monday.'

'What time?'

'In the morning.'

'How convenient,' he said, 'when the tapes are due to be released at midday.' He shook his head. 'You aren't going anywhere yet, but we shall speak later. There are still a couple of hours till sunlight and you should get some sleep. I would prefer to speak when you are properly rested. Your laughter in the face of something so serious is concerning. That sunstroke you mentioned perhaps?'

'I didn't have sunstroke,' she finally admitted.

'I know.'

'I think my drink might have been spiked.'

He said nothing.

'And I'm not tired,' Maggie said. 'Far from it.'

'But you have had such a long day,' he said, 'out on the yacht, entertaining my brother, and then your star-gazing trip…'

His words dripped sarcasm but that didn't faze Maggie in the least.

'You forgot to add being kidnapped,' Maggie said, as if he'd missed adding milk to the shopping list!

He didn't smile.

Ilyas didn't even *almost* smile.

There was no move to his features, at least none that she could see. 'What did you expect to happen?' he asked. 'You are blackmailing the house of al-Razim. Did you think we would merely transfer the funds?'

'I don't know what you're talking about.'

He looked down at the photos she held in her hands. 'How long were you alone with him?'

'A couple of hours.'

Now Ilyas knew she was lying. He well knew Hazin's reputation and he could see how easily he might be framed. In fact, Ilyas had warned him over and over to be careful so as to avoid a scandal such as this.

He accepted, though, that this Maggie might be innocent at some level and might not have known it was all a set-up.

'When you slept with my brother—'

'I've told you,' Maggie shouted now, but it was like screaming into the wind; her words simply swallowed. 'Nothing happened.'

'Oh, please.' He completely dismissed that notion. 'What were you doing, idling the hours away with my brother alone in the cabin?'

'We were talking.'

He gave a mocking laugh. 'I wasn't aware my brother

was such a good conversationalist,' Ilyas said. 'So tell me, what were you discussing?'

Maggie didn't answer.

It had been a private conversation.

She had told Hazin that she was feeling a bit flat, he had asked why, and she had mentioned it was the anniversary of her mother's death. The conversation had gone from there.

She looked now at Hazin's elder brother and knew that what had been said had never been meant for Ilyas to hear.

'I'm not involved,' she said, instead of answering him.

'You *are* involved, and heavily so, in an attempt to bring down my brother.' He waved his hand in rude dismissal and addressed the maidens. 'Take her out.'

Maggie was led away and taken to an area where a large vessel was filled with water. There, the maidens pulled the photos from her hands and moved to undress her.

'Leave me!' she shouted, but the maids persisted so she shouted it again and fought against them.

Ilyas heard the fear in her voice and closed his eyes. His intention had been that the maidens assist her, but the note in her voice made him accept she did not understand that.

'Get off me,' Maggie shouted, and then they halted, only not because of her orders.

She heard his voice call out something and the women moved away. As they did so she could see concern in their expressions.

One said something and pointed to a curtain as she left.

Alone, Maggie stood trying to gather her thoughts

and mute her own terror. When she pulled back the curtain, she saw that it was a sleeping area lit by lanterns.

It was far more lavish than the one from which she had been hauled.

It was actually far more lavish than any she had known.

On the plump bed there lay a muslin slip that, when she examined it, Maggie guessed was intended for her to sleep in.

There was a huge mirror against one of the walls and Maggie looked at herself.

Her hair and clothes were full of sand and she could perhaps see why the maidens and even the Sheikh himself might have decided that a bath and a change of clothes might be in order.

Sheikh?

He was also the crown prince.

Her mind swept back to the conversation she had had with Hazin and what she had gleaned from it about his fractured family.

Ilyas was next in line and the future king.

And he thought she had made a sex tape with his brother?

And what did Suzanne have to do with it all?

She thought of the many times that Suzanne had borrowed her phone, and in the mirror she could see the terror in her eyes as she started to put it all together. She fought to stay calm.

Maggie pulled out her phone but she couldn't get it to turn on, let alone find a signal.

Like her, it was covered in sand.

She was in trouble, Maggie knew.

Serious trouble.

Now she was actually glad of the chance for some space, though certainly she was in no mood to make herself presentable.

But she did need time to think.

Her eyes stung from being sandblasted and her mouth was terribly dry but she ignored the jug and goblet by the bed.

Maggie was certain now that her drink earlier had been spiked and there was no way she would risk it again.

Instead she headed back into the bathing area and, more to calm herself than anything, she finally undressed, got into the bath and tried to work out what on earth to do.

Speak to him.

First she must calm down, and then rationally explain what must have happened, or rather what hadn't.

It took for ever to get the sand out of her hair and she could see the merit of the maidens helping as alone she attempted to pour a heavy jug of water to rinse off.

She was terribly thirsty but had been warned about the water so many times that she chose not to risk the bathwater. Instead, she wrapped herself in a large towel, headed into the sleeping area, and pulled on the slip. She could hear her teeth chattering, though not from the cold desert night, for it was warm in the tent. She climbed into bed and felt her body sink in. She lay there in silence and stared at the billowing ceiling. Her eyes were heavy and scratchy from lack of sleep.

They would notice she was gone in the morning and come looking for her, Maggie attempted to reassure herself.

But she had been told that they did not venture further into the desert without the permission of the king.

And she was stuck with his elder son.

Would anyone even notice her missing?

Probably not.

And, even if they did, surely they would be looking for Suzanne?

The panic she had felt since being grabbed was suddenly replaced by a feeling of loneliness.

Would anyone actually miss her?

Maybe Paul would just assume she wasn't coming back after all. Would he really check with the authorities if she didn't show up for work next week?

There was Flo, her good friend. But Flo was busy with work and her family, as well as her disastrous love life. They weren't in constant touch. Perhaps if she heard nothing, Flo would simply assume that Maggie had extended her holiday.

It might be weeks, Maggie realised, until anyone actually noticed she was gone.

She told herself she was being ridiculous, but it was a silent fear that plagued her at times.

That she could disappear unnoticed.

There was no centre to her world.

Maggie did her best to shrug off the dark thoughts that slunk in.

The sound of bells had her sitting up, and in came the maidens with a tray.

'La,' Maggie said and told them no.

She did not want to be served with refreshments!

'La!' She said again, only more loudly, and again they retreated to the sound of distancing bells.

Curious, she got up and peeked out and saw that the

corridor was also lined with a strip of bells that they must run their hands along to indicate their approach.

Satisfied with her new knowledge, she retrieved the photos she had left in the wash area and got back into bed to examine them.

Not the one of Hazin.

She turned that face down on the floor and looked at the others. Suddenly she was aware she was not alone.

Maggie looked up and saw *him* standing there with the tray she had refused.

'What happened to the bells?' she asked, by way of greeting.

'I don't have to use them,' he said, but then surprisingly accepted her boundary. 'In future I shall.'

'Hopefully there shan't be a reason for you to come in here again,' she said, but immediately felt guilty about her tone after he had been polite and kind.

She could see now that the maidens had only been trying to help and he had been right to suggest she needed to rest.

But he deserved no downgrading of her anger and she shot him a look with her eyes.

Ilyas did not flinch.

He found her a curious mix. She was resigned yet defiant; accepting of her situation while making her own protests.

'You need to eat,' he said.

'No, I don't,' Maggie said, and lay down, speaking with closed eyes. 'A human can go three weeks without food.'

'Very well, but you haven't had a drink since you arrived. We are in the desert...'

'I'm very aware of my location,' Maggie snapped.

'Suzanne.'

She didn't answer to the call of a name that wasn't hers.

'Maggie.'

Her eyes blazed with rage as they opened to his. 'I am taking nothing from you. How do I know what you've put in it?'

'I'm not going to drug you, Maggie,' he said. 'You can trust me.'

'I can't remember where I heard it, but I do seem to recall someone saying never trust a man who kidnaps you in the dead of the night and brings you to his desert tent.'

Maggie stared at his impassive face and realised she had better enlighten him. 'That's sarcasm, by the way.'

'I'm aware of that.'

He filled the goblet and, uninvited, sat on the bed beside her. She lay there, tense and stiff, as he proceeded to drink it down. She could see the movement of his throat as he swallowed and it made her feel oddly weak. 'See,' he proclaimed when it was done, 'there is nothing in it.'

'You might have a high tolerance...'

He smiled.

Not a smile that could go on a dental commercial and perhaps not a smile that many would ever see, but she did observe the slight twitch of his lips that were moistened from the drink.

There was a sudden tsunami warning beneath her belly button. The covers remained, yet it felt as if everything had swept back, leaving her feeling raw and exposed. She lay there, oh, so aware of him, while trying her hardest not to be.

Oh, why, oh, why did she have to find him so impossibly attractive? When every other man left her lukewarm at best, why did this one ignite her on sight?

Why couldn't she have an ugly kidnapper with a hook for a hand and snaggle teeth?

And why couldn't he smell of body odour instead of the exotic, tangy, clean fragrance that she breathed in now?

'Drink,' he said, and replaced the vessel on the table after refilling it. But still Maggie refused to comply.

'When am I going to be freed?'

'No one is going anywhere,' he told her. 'The simoom is fast approaching, so no helicopter can land. For now, you need to have something to drink. I can assure you it is safe.'

'I'm supposed to trust you?' Maggie checked.

'You have to drink,' Ilyas said. 'So I shan't be leaving until you do.'

'That's your choice,' Maggie said. She lay on the silk pillows and closed her eyes, all the while knowing there wasn't the remotest chance of resting with him so close.

The assault on her senses was just as violent with her eyes closed.

More so perhaps.

For now, away from the intensity of those amazing eyes, she could focus on the notes of his scent and the feel of him sitting close to her thigh.

Yes, the feel, for though he sat a respectable distance away there was an awareness so acute that she might soon have to roll to her side just to escape it.

'Maggie.'

He called her by her name but she ignored him.

'I'm not asking you now,' he said, 'I'm telling you.'

'Oh, well, in that case…' Maggie said, and opening her eyes she lifted her hand towards the goblet, but instead of picking it up and doing as she'd been *told*, very deliberately she knocked it from the bedside so that it fell to the carpeted floor.

She was like a cat, Ilyas thought as her defiant eyes met his.

'I shan't be drinking anything,' Maggie said. 'Especially given that the last time I accepted a beverage with an al-Razim close by I ended up being framed.'

Ilyas looked at her for a very long time and knew her words were sincere. If she was telling the truth about her drink being spiked then she had every right to be suspicious now.

Yet it would soon be sunrise and she had been taken just after midnight.

The desert was no place to forego nourishment.

He picked up the vessel from the floor and refilled it again as she lay there staring up at him. Her red hair was splayed out on the pillow and as his hand moved towards her she flinched, but then in a very thorough motion he sat her up.

Maggie's response was not ladylike; she struggled, though it was to no avail. Ilyas put the goblet to her mouth and he poured. Though she fought, he was stronger. But that was not the reason she gave in—suddenly they were close, so close, and there was the ragged sound of his breathing, the *feel* of his hand on the back of her head, and the overwhelming sensation that Ilyas was near.

It was safer to swallow.

Ilyas felt the change too.

One moment he was fighting to get her to take a

drink, the next he was fighting with himself not to kiss her. But thankfully Maggie suddenly complied and took in some of the fluid, though most of it she already wore down her neck and chest.

He was sitting on the bed, holding her, and in that brief tussle everything had changed. His grip on her loosened and Maggie was aware of her body and his in a way that she had never been before.

'There, I've drunk it,' she said, though her voice came out wrong, for even the cords in her throat were strung taut by his touch.

And he too fought for normalcy, and to remember the reason he had come in here.

He released Maggie and was about to refill the goblet but then he changed his mind, for the spilled liquid had wet the fabric of her slip, making it translucent. It clung to one of her breasts, the nipple puckered and taut. Ilyas's voice, when he found it, was brusque. 'I have no issue doing that hourly so, if you would prefer that I didn't play nursemaid, I suggest you take another long drink before you sleep.'

He stalked out and she sat there with a sweet taste on her lips and feeling breathless from his touch.

And then, a beat too late, for he must have just remembered her request, she heard the sound of bells as he departed.

CHAPTER FIVE

THERE WAS A brief twilight zone when Maggie awoke.

A moment where she lay, rested by sleep, but while unaware of her surroundings.

It didn't last.

Maggie was fully awake now, aware of her predicament but less fearful.

Clearly she wouldn't be allowed to die of thirst in the desert!

He had taken certain care and that was reassuring to know.

She also had the truth on her side.

Maggie lay there listening to the screaming winds and stared at the tented wall that did not move. She wondered how it could be so still when clearly they were deep in the simoom.

She could hear the sounds and sizzles from a Berber kitchen and, far from lasting three weeks, Maggie doubted she could last three minutes more without food, for she was suddenly ravenous.

She pulled back the sheets and sat up, noticing that a robe had been put out for her. The fabric was a very pale willow-green crushed velvet. As soon as Maggie put on the robe she knew that she had never worn real velvet before. It felt like warm silk and though modest it clung a little to her. There were pretty slippers too that were crusted with jewels.

Her hair was damp and knotted and she ran her fingers through it more from habit than to look *presentable.*

The air was fragrant with spices as she headed out and she really was terribly hungry but determined not to show it.

He was seated on the floor at a low table and one of the maidens that Maggie had shooed away previously gave her a nice smile.

A little shy and embarrassed at how she had treated her, Maggie returned it.

Ilyas gestured for her to take a seat while trying not to notice just how amazing she looked. The sleep had served her well. There was colour in her cheeks and her eyes were less wary. Certainly he did his best not to notice how stunning her figure looked in the robe, or that it was a similar shade to the bikini she had worn in the photos.

Ilyas wanted her, and he was more than used to having his wants met. He had to remember that there were more important issues than that now.

And he was not one to sleep with the enemy.

'How did you sleep?' he enquired.

'Terribly,' Maggie lied.

'You appeared unconscious when the maids checked on you.'

'I was just resting my eyes,' Maggie said, then she smiled, though not at him, because there was a flash of a long-ago memory of her mother saying that when Maggie would catch her dozing.

Here, in the desert, she felt as if her mother was close.

'What time is it?' she asked.

'Seven,' he said, and then nodded to the maid to remove the lids from various tajines.

The dishes all looked delectable.

'I have been thinking about what you said,' Ilyas told her once the maiden had left. 'If your drink was indeed tampered with then I understand your concerns about the food and refreshments—however, you cannot go without either.'

'It's fine.' Maggie sighed and tried to sound wearily magnanimous. 'I really don't have much choice but to eat.'

'Quite.'

'So I *shall* have breakfast.'

'Dinner,' he corrected. 'It is seven in the evening, not the morning. According to the maidens you were also *resting your eyes* when breakfast and lunch were served.'

Oh, she was so embarrassed! She was about to make some quip about the tea he had forced on her being a sedative, but Maggie knew that had nothing to do with her sleeping for so long.

'I trust you were comfortable, then?' he checked. 'Given how long you slept.'

She could hardly deny it, but instead of answering she filled a goblet and took a drink. Ilyas offered her a flat bread which Maggie took and then covered with some meat.

She took a bite. It really was delicious, spicy yet sweet, and the meat was so tender it simply melted on her tongue. It was hard to swallow, though, for she could feel his eyes on her and Maggie knew there was much to be discussed.

'How are you involved with Suzanne?' he asked.

'I met her while travelling,' Maggie told him, and decided it was time to be more honest and stop covering for Suzanne. 'We were both rooming at the same hostel. Last night she left for Dubai. I believe she was meeting her boyfriend there.'

'Do you know him too?'

Maggie shook her head. 'She just said she was catching up with Glen.'

'How long ago did you meet her?'

'A couple of months ago. We worked at the same bar for a few weeks and then we parted ways. We caught up again here in Zayrinia but it was by chance.'

'You're sure of that?'

'No,' she admitted, for despite her mammoth sleep she had also been doing a lot of thinking. 'I did say to her a while back that I had been hoping to come here near the end of my trip but I never gave dates. I had to save up—it's been a working holiday,' she explained.

'What do you do back home?'

'I work in a café,' Maggie said.

'For how long?'

'Since I was fifteen, though I was just part time then, so…' She did the maths. 'Nine years.'

'You must like it.'

'I do. The staff are great and it's more like…' She hesitated. 'Well, my boss is like family, really.'

'Good,' he said, and she liked it that he did.

All too often people asked why she didn't look for something different or assumed she must be bored working there, but the truth was she was more than happy with her job. The café had been the most constant thing in her life. 'It's a chocolate café.'

'A chocolate café?' Ilyas checked.

'Iced chocolate, hot chocolate, chocolate cake, chocolate biscuits, chocolate everything.'

'You must be sick of chocolate?'

'Never.' Maggie smiled. 'And believe me when I say I've tried to be.' Then she stopped smiling. 'Is this relevant?'

'Not really,' Ilyas said, and then he frowned, but at his own lapse, for usually he stayed very much on topic. Yet it was pleasant speaking to her, interesting finding out more about this rather intriguing woman. 'You said you have worked while overseas. Doing what?'

'More cafés.' Maggie shrugged. 'And a few bars. That's where I met Suzanne.'

'So how did you end up on my brother's yacht?'

'Suzanne said she had a plus-one invitation for a snorkelling trip.'

'A snorkelling trip for tourists aboard the royal yacht?' Ilyas's response was wry and then he met her eyes. 'That was sarcasm, by the way.'

'I know that,' Maggie responded, and then sighed. 'And merited. I knew something was off the moment I saw it.'

'Yet you boarded?'

'Yes,' Maggie said. 'I'm trying to be less cynical.'

'Why would you do that?'

'Because I'm aware that it's somewhat a fault of mine.'

'I would call it an asset.' And to prove his own cynicism he questioned her further. 'So you and Hazin spent the afternoon merely talking?'

'*We're* merely talking,' Maggie pointed out.

'It took rather a lot of effort to get to this point.'

She was not deterred by his tone. 'I spoke readily then because your brother didn't kidnap me in the middle of the night.' She sweetly smiled and then helped herself to more of the delicious food. 'In fact, I ended up in his cabin by mistake. Or I thought I had. He was very nice about it. I wasn't enjoying the trip and neither was he.'

'Why?'

Maggie's lips pursed; she did not want to reveal anything that Hazin had told her. She and Hazin were far from friends but, still, that conversation had been private and certainly not for his brother's ears.

'Why weren't you enjoying yourself?' Ilyas asked, and his interest surprised both of them.

He wanted to know, and now he *really* wanted to know, for colour came to her cheeks.

'I felt like a tart,' Maggie said. 'And, despite what you may think of me, I'm not one.' He just looked at her. 'I knew I was way out of my depth and when I felt sick all of a sudden I was very happy to escape and lie down. I had no idea it was your brother's cabin.'

'There were cameras planted.' Ilyas revealed some of what the messages had said. 'Anything that happened between the two of you will be there for all to see.'

'Then make a cup of tea and prepare for an early night,' Maggie said. 'We were just talking.'

She did flush a little, though, embarrassed and worried that what Hazin had said might have been captured. He had spoken about his family and, given his status, he would not want the world to know what had been said.

Of course, Ilyas misinterpreted her blush as one of guilt.

Still, no matter what had taken place between Maggie and Hazin, there was one thing he could not work out.

'I don't understand why they would choose you.' He frowned.

'Am I not to your brother's usual taste?' Maggie said, and then it was she who frowned. 'They?'

'These people work in groups. And what I said has nothing to do with looks and appeal.' Though he could well understand if that were the case! 'I meant I don't understand why they would choose someone as damned defiant and argumentative as you.'

'I'm not with you,' Maggie said, and then she laughed. 'Well, I get that I'm no pushover but I'm not sure what you mean about being chosen.'

'You don't seem to be the sort to be so readily taken in.'

'I'm not,' Maggie said, but then she hesitated. A tiny curl of a conversation had started unfurling in her mind and she tried to dismiss it, telling herself that she would think about it later, when she was away from the scrutiny of his gaze. But Ilyas had already noticed her hesitation.

'Tell me.'

'It's nothing.' She shook her head and then, suddenly not hungry, she pushed away the plate. 'I'm done talking.'

If anything, Maggie felt a little sick.

So much so that she excused herself and headed back to her room and sat on the bed.

The pictures lay scattered on the floor and instead

of looking at them she buried her head in her hands and let out a low moan.

Until now it had all seemed like a mistake, a misunderstanding that Maggie had been oddly confident would soon be cleared up.

It had buoyed her. In fact, the absurdity of her situation had placated her.

Now she was starting to see that she had been set up by Suzanne.

Used.

And she knew now why she had been chosen.

She heard the sound of bells and guessed that Ilyas had followed her. 'Maggie?'

He spoke her name before he parted the curtain and Ilyas saw her sitting on the bed as if she had just been told bad news.

'What did you just remember?' he asked.

'Nothing.'

'You seem upset.'

She didn't look at him. In fact, she gave a small derisive laugh. 'What do you expect?'

'You've remembered something.'

She had.

'Tell me.'

Ilyas wasn't asking merely to solve the situation. He wasn't even asking to work out the mystery with his brother or to get his family out of trouble.

He was asking because it was clear that she was hurt.

And, in his eternal quest for information, usually he didn't care about such matters.

Now, though, he did. And so he spoke more kindly than usual and came and sat on the bed beside her.

Maggie didn't jump like a scalded cat, but only because his presence didn't feel like a threat now. And though, as she sat there, she told herself to maintain her anger with him, that he did not deserve any lowering in her rage, she was starting to see that he was right to be angry about what had happened to his brother and the demands that had been made.

It wasn't a simple mix-up.

'I think I've been set up,' Maggie admitted. 'I can't check, my phone's not working…' She gestured to it and Ilyas picked it up and tried to turn it on. 'Suzanne kept borrowing it.'

'I'll have it cleaned,' Ilyas said, and pocketed it. 'What else have you remembered?'

'It's probably nothing,' she said, and then gave in. 'But I don't think so.' Maggie was piecing it all together, even as he sat by her side. 'I told you that Suzanne and I worked together?'

He nodded.

'We went out for drinks a few times. I guess we became friends. Or at least I thought we had. One time, I can't even remember exactly what we were talking about, but I said that I wanted to be home by the end of summer.'

'Which is now.'

Maggie nodded. 'My boss, Paul, wants me to go back to the café, but apart from that I had no real reason to rush back.'

'What about your home?'

'I don't have one,' Maggie said. 'I just rented a room in a flat. I told Suzanne the same and that no one was really expecting me back.'

'No one?' he checked.

And she should possibly not be telling him this, Maggie realised, but she was starting to see that he wasn't the enemy or the one taking advantage of her status.

That had been Suzanne.

'My boss and my friend, Flo, know my plans.'

And he waited for her to explain further.

'But I don't have any family, not really. My mother was single and she died when I was seven. She lost touch with her family when she was pregnant with me—they were all in Ireland anyway.'

'Who raised you after your mother died?'

'I was in and out of care homes and there were a couple of foster homes but they didn't work out. Apart from friends, there's no one,' Maggie admitted. 'I guess Suzanne realised there was no one to miss me.'

She could see how it had happened now.

All those questions that Maggie had thought insensitive at the time had been Suzanne digging for information.

'I should have listened to my instincts,' Maggie said. 'I knew something wasn't right at the time. I just didn't know what—Suzanne had me pegged as disposable.'

'Well, she was wrong.'

The conviction in his voice had her look at him.

'You don't know that.'

'I think I do,' Ilyas said. 'You said that you have friends?'

'Of course,' Maggie said, 'not many, but…' She didn't really know how to explain, but she tried. 'I don't get close to people very easily.'

'I heard that if, apart from family, you can count on one hand your true friends and people you have truly loved then you go to your grave a lucky man.'

'I'm not a man.'

'I know,' Ilyas said, and smiled, for he certainly did! 'Go on...' he said, and he took her furled hand. 'Name one.'

'Flo,' Maggie said immediately.

'How did you meet?'

'She started to come into the café when she was a nursing student. She's a midwife now.'

'And you're good friends?'

Maggie nodded. 'Very. Flo's the best.' And she watched as he unfurled one of her fingers.

'Who else?'

'Paul.' Was it her imagination or did his hand hesitate a touch when she said Paul's name? 'He's my boss,' she explained. 'But we get on really well.' She watched his hand on hers as she elaborated. 'And his wife.'

His fingers relaxed into hers. 'I was their bridesmaid,' she told him. 'Though Kerry, his wife, doesn't quite count as a finger,' Maggie said. 'So that's two.' She looked at the hand he held in his. 'I've got other friends, of course, but...'

'Two is excellent,' he said. 'I would hope you have many years to find the other three. I am sure that if I kept you here in the desert you would be very much missed.'

He wasn't going to keep her, though.

Maggie knew he believed her and she knew she was safe.

'How many fingers do you have?' Maggie asked, but he didn't readily respond. She was more than curious, and not just about friends, for she wondered if there was a woman in his life.

'I don't count people on fingers,' Ilyas said, 'for I will one day be king.'

'I don't understand.'

'I have shoulders.'

'So there are separate rules for you?' Maggie asked, and her question was slightly mocking.

'Of course there are,' he said, and then moved the subject back to what they had been discussing. 'Maggie, you are far from disposable. I would imagine your friends miss you very much and are looking forward to you coming home.'

'Really?'

He nodded. 'I am sure that others find your company very pleasing.'

It was an odd thing to say and it begged a question. 'You don't?'

'I find it disconcerting,' Ilyas said. 'But pleasing too, though disconcerting would be my first choice of word.'

'And mine,' Maggie admitted. 'I mean, if I had to describe you.'

They were looking right at each other and their mouths were so close she could feel his warmth.

'But pleasing?' Ilyas checked.

'For the most part,' Maggie agreed.

'What about this part?'

She knew what his question meant and that he was about to kiss her.

It was odd, but on the very few dates she had been on, the whole time had been spent wondering if it was time for the kiss. And then being disappointed when it was.

None of that applied to Ilyas.

She had known he would kiss her.

Not just in the moment before he did but for perhaps a thousand moments before he had.

It was as if their kiss had been born when his hand had gone behind her head and he had forced her to drink, or even a little before then, for that kiss had felt inevitable.

Necessary.

Yes, his kiss had been waiting for her since then.

And it didn't disappoint, for Ilyas knew her wants better than she.

Until his hand held her face and his lips found hers, Maggie hadn't known that it was not a tentative kiss she required, but one that was planned.

And plan he did, for Ilyas cupped her cheeks and looked at her mouth till the flesh there tingled with both want and anticipation. The kiss he gave was not to a closed mouth, for he waited for her lips to part and, when they did, he gave her hungry mouth the firm weight of his.

His mouth moved with hers and the scent of him was enticing. She found that her hands moved to his chest and then upwards so that her arms linked around his neck as she accepted the sensual bliss of his tongue.

This was a kiss, Maggie thought, for it was exactly as it should be. The caress of his tongue was welcomed by hers and the taste of them together was divine.

There was no wandering of his hands; they stayed soft on her cheeks. The only contact he gave was the scratch of his jaw and the full attention of his mouth.

Maggie found herself aching to be held more fiercely, to know completely his embrace, yet he kissed her as if they had all the time in the world.

They *had* all the time he required, Maggie suddenly thought, for she was, after all, his prisoner and at that crude realisation she pulled back.

Ilyas had anticipated that she would—the attraction between them was undeniable, yet he had known she would fight it.

She reminded him of a young, wary falcon and knew that patience was required here. And that was the reason he had taken things no further, even though desire coursed through them both.

Her breath was ragged and her eyes blinked rapidly as he continued to hold her face. Their lips were moist and their chests were close to touching.

He dropped contact then and she felt the heat in her cheeks as he stared at her. She fought not to reach for more of his kiss or to lean into him, but then the choice was removed, for he stood.

Maggie opened her mouth to speak, but then closed it, for she didn't know what to say.

It was best that he leave as she needed to think and she could not do that with Ilyas close by.

'I'll go,' he told her.

'Please.' She looked at him. 'That was a mistake.'

'It didn't feel like one,' Ilyas answered. 'It still doesn't.'

Clearly he hadn't read the bedding-a-virgin etiquette manual, for he took her hand and pressed it into his robe. She could feel how hard he was.

She went to pull her hand away but he held her tight there and she gave in with a very weak protest because he felt magnificent. Maggie didn't resist when he pressed her palm in.

'Whatever happened to flirting?' Maggie asked, and her normal voice had completely gone, for her words croaked through a throat that felt impossibly dry.

Elsewhere she was not.

'I don't need to flirt,' he told her. He released her

from his grip, though for a telling moment her hand remained before she reclaimed it.

'Maybe you do,' Maggie said.

'I don't think so.' He was, after all, a man who summoned sex with a bell. 'Come out when you are ready.'

Maggie wasn't sure that she would ever be ready, yet their kiss had left her wanting more and Ilyas knew exactly that.

It was the reason he left—he wanted her willing when she returned to his arms.

CHAPTER SIX

MAGGIE TRIED TO deny the pull to go out there.

She had never come close to this level of want before.

In truth, she never allowed herself to get close to anyone for fear of being taken in by promises and lies.

Ilyas didn't lie.

Far from it—he made absolutely no apology for his desire.

And that was all it was, Maggie knew.

Sexual desire.

She wondered what he would think if he knew that just the touch of him through a robe was further than she had ever gone before.

She lay there and the music grew louder, filling the sleeping area and seemingly plucking at her taut nerves, and she knew that she would never again know a lover like him.

There was something raw and carnal about him that had her stomach pulling tight, even at first sight.

She could not take a full breath when thinking about him, let alone when he was present.

He made her aware of her own body, and whenever he was near, Maggie felt herself flare to the imperceptible attention he gave it.

Imperceptible, for his eyes did not drift over her and there was nothing that made her feel uncomfortable as there had been on the yacht.

Quite simply, he turned her on in a way no one ever had.

And that had started long before their kiss.

The music throbbed and her desire was deep, but as she climbed out of the bed and caught sight of her reflection in the mirror, Maggie knew she could no more walk in there and simply take up where they had left off than she could fly to the moon.

Oh, she was naïve in body but not in mind, and she knew there could never be more than their time here in the desert. But, while she accepted he was a ruler, it did not mean she could not make her own demands.

And she would tell him so.

She stood barefoot at the entrance to the main area, where he lay on his side, with fruits laid out on the carpeted floor. She told him what she had decided.

'I shan't sleep with someone I don't know.'

'Then we shan't be together,' Ilyas said.

'So no one can get to know you?'

'Of course not.'

'Because you're too important?' she mocked.

'No, but my secrets are.'

She looked at him, and after a moment his haughty face softened a touch and he gestured for her to join him. She hesitated.

'It's okay,' Ilyas said. 'We don't have to do anything, neither shall we speak of sex or Suzanne…'

He was the most direct person she had ever met and yet he had her spinning.

Wanting.

Needing.

Maggie tentatively knelt and reached for a goblet, confused by her own thoughts, for it felt as if he had cast a spell on her. When he spoke, his voice was normal, and she attempted conversation as if there was no turmoil, yet all the time she felt as if she had been set loose on a wild sea and holding nothing but a ship's rail.

'Let's call a truce,' he suggested. 'We are stuck here until tomorrow at least. The centre of the storm is close.'

'How come the walls of the tent don't move?' Maggie asked something that had been niggling at her. Just a small thing, but it was far safer to voice that than anything else on her mind.

She looked up at the ceiling, which billowed gently, but apart from the noise of the increasing wind one would never know they were in the midst of a fierce storm.

'Because we are in the inner tent,' Ilyas explained. 'There is an outer layer that takes the force of the storm. If the walls start to move, we are in trouble.'

Maggie was already in trouble, for it felt as if the ground was moving beneath her. Just the low growl of his voice had her fighting not to inch her way a little closer to him.

'What was your accommodation like on the tour?' he asked.

'Well, put it this way—there was no inner tent!'

She liked it that he smiled.

'There are issues with some of the operators,' Ilyas said.

'I could have told you that.'

And she proceeded to tell him how the trip to the desert had started out a little bit shoddy and rather contrived.

'They want to take the tourists deeper into the desert,' Ilyas explained, 'but the Bedouins have opposed it.'

'What are they opposed to?'

'They resist all change,' Ilyas said.

'There's surely a lot the tour operators could do without upsetting them.'

'Such as?'

And he surprised himself now, for usually he would not ask an outsider.

'I don't know offhand,' Maggie admitted, and then smiled. 'You'd have to ask them!'

'Pardon?'

The wind howled outside and with the *quanoon* playing, conversation was proving difficult.

'I said, you'd have to ask them.'

Ilyas stared at her. Her response surprised him, not that he let it show, but it had been so attuned to his own thoughts that he was a little taken aback. He wanted to hear more from Maggie. 'Come here,' he said, and patted a cushion that was nearer to him.

Even as she moved closer the truce remained, for he made no move to touch her. Instead, he asked for more of her thoughts.

'Maybe don't advertise it as stargazing,' she suggested. 'Especially when the operators know there isn't a chance of stars. It could be a nice bonus but the trip itself could be enough. I know that I loved sitting around the campfire and hearing the stories.'

'What did they tell you?'

'About a river under the palace that still runs red.' She turned and looked at his expression for a reaction but Ilyas gave nothing away so she spoke on. 'How a prince died of a broken heart and how it's still bleeding to this day.'

He just stared.

'Is it true?' Maggie asked.

'Are you asking if it's true that thousands of years later his heart lies still bleeding?' He saw her sag a touch at his dismissal. 'Anyway, if the prince was so weak as to die of a broken heart then he probably did his country a favour.'

'Love doesn't make you weak,' Maggie countered.

'Of course it does. He should have been focusing on the job in hand.'

'You're not very romantic.'

'Not in the least.'

'So it's not true, then?'

'I never said that.' He was trying not to smile at her obvious frustration. 'Tell me what else they said.'

The wind was swirling outside. They were surely nearing the eye of the storm, for they kept having to lean in just to hear each other. 'They told us about the palace, and how it was built on ruins that were once a harem. How the noise of the wind is really the sounds of debauchery crossing time…'

He laughed.

It was low and it was deep and just so unexpected that she almost joined in, but Maggie had enjoyed hearing the legends and let out a small wail.

'I liked it,' she admitted. 'Is it all a lie?'

'Not a complete lie,' he said. 'The palace isn't built on ruins—there is a huge *hammam* underground and a large network of caves.' He told her about the caves and the fountains and how, though underground, some of the cave entrances were exposed to the desert. 'There is a ledge at one entrance,' Ilyas said. 'No one else is permitted there other than me. There, it is like standing in the middle of the sky,' Ilyas said. 'Sometimes when it has been a difficult day and I stand looking out, it feels as if the ground has disappeared from beneath me and I stand alone in the sky.'

The way he described it in his rich, smooth voice made her shiver. Their heads moved closer, though not so much to hear better, more to be near each other. She could feel the warmth from his skin on her cheek and her mouth felt too heavy for her face.

'In days of old,' Ilyas told her, 'the early leaders would meet at the waterfall to discuss business and the problems with the Bedouins. Back then it was the closest they could get to the desert. Today, the royals rule the entire land but within the palace are the stone benches where they first sat. After their meetings they would retire to the *hammam*. In time, the palace was built over and around it. First it was small, and now it's the masterpiece that it is.'

'So there once was a harem?'

'There still is,' Ilyas said. 'I would guess that the debauched sounds that carry across the desert are more likely to be current ones than ghosts of the past...'

She pulled her head back and looked at him. Her face was on fire.

'And do you...?' She swallowed, not really sure how to word the question that she had in mind.

'Do I what?' he asked. They were still close enough that he could actually feel the heat from her blush and then he understood what she asked. 'Of course.'

He watched as the blush rose and lit like a flame and he saw her eyes flash in anger.

'You have the gall to haul me here on the assumption I slept with your brother, when all the time—'

'You were brought here because it was believed you were blackmailing the palace and threatening to damage the reputation of my brother,' Ilyas pointed out.

'Reputation?' she gave an incredulous laugh. 'If the people knew what you were up to...'

'You think if the people knew that their crown prince had a healthy sexual appetite they would be shocked?'

Her lips pursed.

'The harem is beautiful, the women are looked after and are free to leave if they please. There is no entrapment and certainly no desire to share the encounter with anyone else for personal gain. It is about mutual pleasure.'

'Mutual?' she sneered.

Ilyas said nothing. Instead he carefully selected a fig from the selection of fruit and took up a knife, separating the fruit into two and offering her a piece.

'No, thank you.'

'Please,' Ilyas said. 'They are exceptional right now.'

His hand, unlike hers, was absolutely steady and after a moment she took the fig and then bit in.

Ilyas was right—it was utterly delicious, rich yet sweet, syrupy and golden.

'It's wonderful.'

'Good.'

He took a mouthful and she watched as he chewed and then he nodded in agreement. 'Of course, had the fruit been damaged I would not have offered you that part. I would have selected another, or taken that piece for myself. There is pleasure in watching another enjoy. If not, then you might as well eat by yourself.'

She replaced the uneaten portion of fig on the pretty plate before her.

Maggie knew he was referring to sex, and that he had just chastised her for daring to suggest that his lovers derived little pleasure.

The topic, though, was far out of her league.

'Perhaps I don't like figs.'

'Then don't eat it. I would far rather you spit it out than feign enjoyment,' he said. 'Cheap fruit, on the other hand, is another matter—looks good on the outside, but underneath it is either rotten or tasteless.'

Maggie knew for sure they were no longer talking about fruit.

'Alluring,' he added, for though they had agreed a truce he simply could not bear the thought of what she might have done.

'I would not know how to lure and seduce, even if it were my job,' Maggie cried.

'Please,' he scoffed, though his meaning was lost on her, for Ilyas had the proof before his eyes of the temptation she was—and he was not referring to his brother.

But his comment had burst Maggie's temper. 'You should be having this conversation with Hazin. If he is so bloody corrupt that you assume this to be true, then what the hell are you doing, running around cleaning up after him?'

'Leave it!'

'No.'

Maggie had heard enough.

'Why do you blame me as you sit there defending him? Why do you run around cleaning up the mess he makes?'

'Because someone has to.'

It wasn't just his admission that surprised her but the harsh, bleak tone in which it was delivered.

'Hazin is heading for trouble. You are right, I should just leave him to it but…' He didn't know what to say, for if it had been anyone else, Ilyas would have let them fall.

'You love him.'

She said it as fact but Ilyas shook his head, certain it could not be that. 'I hardly know him. We were never together when we were younger.'

'Never?'

'Not really,' Ilyas said. 'We met for formal occasions but were segregated at other times.' Even as he shook his head he cast his mind back. 'Once, though, there was a mix-up.' He smiled at the memory. 'Hazin's nanny was away and the elder who was supposed to be giving me guidance fell ill. We didn't inform anyone,' Ilyas said, and he smiled at the memory. 'We had a day to run wild.'

'Just a day?'

Ilyas nodded.

'How old were you?'

'Eight or so, maybe seven. We went down past the *hammam* and swam in a cave lake…'

'You could have drowned.'

'We didn't, though,' Ilyas said. 'We played and we laughed and we were brothers for a day. Hazin said that he wished I was king and that we could rule together. He was so young I doubt he even remembers.'

Maggie doubted it too, for from all Hazin had told her he held no happy memories. Hazin had made it clear to Maggie that he considered his brother as cold and as emotionally empty as his parents.

'Even at such a tender age Hazin knew things were wrong,' Ilyas said.

'Wrong?'

He never usually thought of old times and he certainly never spoke of them, yet the conversation with Maggie was soothing rather than unsettling, and the wind made a temporary shield from the world—or it felt as if it did.

'I don't always agree with my father's rule.'

It wasn't a secret as such. Most of the elders knew it and the people of Zayrinia all fervently hoped that Ilyas was merely biding his time until it was his turn to be king.

Still, it should not be said.

Perhaps Maggie did not understand the magnitude of his revelations, Ilyas thought, for she did not swallow nervously and neither did her eyes widen. In fact, she asked a question in the same matter-of-fact way that she had when they had discussed the Bedouin and tourist issue. 'What don't you agree with?'

His eyes narrowed a little at her question and he reminded himself of her status—a woman who might lure and then blackmail a prince.

And then he knew that that was not Maggie. He knew it for sure deep inside him.

'We are a prosperous country,' Ilyas said, 'yet many of the people are poor.'

'Can you do something about it?' she asked.

'Not yet,' Ilyas said, and as she stared deep into his beautiful eyes, Maggie could see they housed a secret.

She could see it dancing on the edges of his stunning gaze, yet he did not allow her to linger and search that path, for he tore his eyes away and told her there was nothing he could do. 'He is king.'

Ilyas pulled at a rope and after a moment a maiden appeared and he gave his orders.

'What did you say to her?' Maggie asked.

'I asked that the musicians play louder.'

It was safer than talking.

'Where are they?' She frowned, looking around.

'In another area,' Ilyas told her. 'They cannot hear us, but we can hear them.'

The music grew louder.

While it halted conversation, it did nothing to dim their desire.

Ilyas looked over and saw that Maggie sat with her eyes closed, drinking in the music as if she were being warmed by the rays of the sun.

A long curl fell across her forehead and he was tempted to move it away. Not so that he could see her better, or because it might irritate her, and perhaps not even for the feel of her hair on his fingers.

Just because.

His hand reached out for no real reason he could find but, as it did, his senses overrode the impulse and he moved his hand back from such an unnecessary touch.

But she turned just in time.

Their eyes met and he could see that she read his action like a book.

'Dance?' Ilyas said.

'I would love to.'

But then sense kicked in.

For he did not dance and certainly he did not sit staring into anyone's eyes. The kiss they had shared had been more tender and intimate than any he had known, and that was not what he usually sought.

Maggie Delaney took up far too much space in his mind and Ilyas knew that he had to pull back, had to somehow eliminate the closeness between them.

And so he quickly amended his request and made out that he had been requesting her to dance *for* him rather than asking her to dance *with* him.

'Go on, then.'

Maggie felt her cheeks flush, even before she registered his words.

Her response to his offer had been immediate and heartfelt, for she had truly thought he was asking her to dance.

Embarrassment prickled—tiny red pokers of heat that flushed her cheeks and spread across her chest.

And unless she wanted to admit her mistake and let Ilyas know that she had jumped at the chance to be held by him, she had to rectify things, and quickly.

And so she stood.

Anger blazed in her green eyes, though she offered him a smile.

She did not dance. Well, not alone.

Or only on rare occasions and certainly not with anyone watching.

But how hard could it be? Maggie thought. She started to sway her hips a little, though she felt an utter fool.

Bastard! Her eyes shouted it, even as she raised her arms above her head as the far more practised woman had done by the campfire on the night she had been taken.

Yes, you utter bastard, she thought as she danced,

because though she might look more like a jester than a dancer it was surely better than admitting her mistake.

But then she couldn't carry on the charade, and she ground to a halt.

'I can't…'

He had been watching her with an inward smile, for he took a certain amount of pleasure in the discipline of denial.

Ilyas gave in to it then and stood.

As he walked over and took her hand, Maggie looked into his eyes.

She knew him better now.

CHAPTER SEVEN

HE LOVED IT that she had tried.

'It looked easy when I was watching the dancers,' Maggie said as he came over.

'It just takes practice,' he told her. He came up behind her and placed both hands on her hips. 'Like this.'

'Like what?' Maggie asked, fighting the urge to lean back on him.

'Stay centred.'

That was terribly easy to say when there wasn't six foot three of sheikh right behind you and holding you extremely low on your hips.

'Now push my right hand away,' he told her.

She tried.

And failed.

'First drop your thigh,' he told her, 'and then push up.'

His palm on her hip bone seared the top of her thigh but somehow Maggie followed his instruction.

'Now my left.'

It was clumsy and nothing like it should be, yet she shifted to the rhythm and Ilyas moved further in so that his face came next to hers.

Now his hand moved to her stomach. *Tell him to stop,*

Maggie thought, because she could not even pretend she was dancing as she fought not to lean back.

'Like this,' Ilyas said, and ground her hips in a circular motion by pressing her back into his pelvis.

Her back was pushing hard against him and she fought to keep her bottom from doing the same.

'Like this,' he told her, and she gave up fighting and even vaguely pretending it was a dance lesson.

And so too did he.

Ilyas lifted her hair and he breathed in her scent, and then his head lowered to her neck and he kissed her pale skin.

The touch of his mouth was soft, yet it shot volts through Maggie that had her neck arch to the side.

His kiss deepened and his tongue was probing on a sensitive area; an involuntary moan escaped from her lips.

Finally, Ilyas pulled her tight in to him.

She could feel his arousal as he swayed her hips but it was far more intimate than a dance.

Her thigh jerked, albeit involuntarily, yet it was the most sensual move she could have made for the reward was Ilyas's return motion.

His breath was ragged and his sensual movements were deliberate; Maggie fought an internal battle to remain standing. If she gave in, she knew she would simply fold over.

'Ilyas,' she breathed, for his kiss was deeper now and moving down from her neck to her shoulder, and his hand pulled the fabric of her robe down her arm.

Still, his other hand remained low on her stomach. His touch was warm and her reaction was scorching.

They moved sensually, his hand now sliding the strap

of her slip down so that her breast was exposed. His fingers were firm and a little rough on her sensitive flesh as his mouth worked like a heated balm on her shoulder.

Her thighs were shaking and pressed hard into him so she could steady herself, but it served only to inflame.

Badly she wanted to turn around and claim the kiss that was surely waiting. His tongue wetted her neck and delivered sensual heat as he kissed up and down.

The music was mesmerising—each pluck of the *quanoon*'s strings seemed to match her internal frenzy. His hand moved from her stomach when she wished it would not, for the subtle pressure was divine. But then Ilyas tore at her slip and robe so that she was naked from the waist up. His hands found their way to her breasts, and they caressed and teased and stroked until she could barely remember her own name.

Maggie was desperate to taste his mouth, so she arched her neck and, finally, their lips met. The kiss they exchanged was deep and served only to increase her desire for him.

He pushed down her robe and slip so they fell to the floor, and as they did she heard him unbuckle the low belt of his robe and the sound of ripping muslin. At last, there was the feel of his naked flesh along the entire length of her body.

His hand grasped the back of her head and pushed it down so that she was exposed to him.

A finger ran the length of her spine and then he cupped the cheek of her buttock. Maggie wriggled to free herself of his hold.

Her fight was not about consent, for she could not want him more.

Maggie just wanted to turn and look at him, so she would remember this moment for ever.

But one of his hands held her in place, the palm putting a subtle pressure on her neck, his other hand holding himself at her entrance. Her fear now was real. 'It's my first time,' she gasped, for, though she was on the edge of orgasm, he would tear her in two, she was sure.

'Good,' he said, with the compassion of an ant, for Ilyas was more than pleased to be her first and he would teach her well.

Yet Ilyas felt her buttocks tense against his skin, and as he nudged inside her he could feel more than virginal resistance, as if the writhing wanton woman was braced for displeasure.

She was gulping in air, and as his arm slipped around her stomach, he realised she was leaning on his solid forearm as if grasping a pool edge.

Torn between desire and fear, Maggie refused to simply close her eyes and go with it.

'Ilyas…' She slipped from his grasp and turned to face him. She stopped, shocked into stillness. It was not the man she had known, for his robe was open and his outstanding body was on full display to her.

Oh, he was exquisite—muscled and strong and glistening. She put a hand up to feel him.

His skin was warm beneath her fingers as she pushed into the wall of his chest. Ilyas took her other hand in his and lowered it so she could feel his hard length.

'Take me slowly,' Maggie said, stroking him with her hand.

Ilyas was far from used to a woman dictating the pace—he was about quick satisfaction, straight to the top, not a lingering, gradual ascent.

His lovers knew that.

But she was not his lover...yet.

Her touch was sublime. Now they were face to face, he shrugged off his robe so they were both fully naked, and then he explored her body as she explored his.

Maggie closed her eyes at his surprisingly tender touch and then, as their mouths met again, the heat of him against her stomach had her mouth tense in a frenzied kiss.

Each bruising action of his lips melded them closer together as they lowered themselves to the floor and both discovered the bliss of unhurried pleasures.

His mouth found her breast and, already tender, he stiffened her nipples to painful peaks with his skilful tongue.

She did not know true bliss, though, until he kissed her down her pale stomach and then parted her legs, kneeling between them and stroking the Titian-red curls.

'Ilyas...' Her voice choked as his tongue first explored her glistening lips, and then probed more deeply and intimately. He lifted her calves over his wide shoulders and she fought again, for she did not know how to relax and sink into the bliss.

'Please,' she begged, trying to raise herself up on her elbows, because this delicious torture was relentless and surely could not be sustained. But he pushed her back down and lifted her hips, taking her with his tongue. Each beat had her writhing.

'You want it slow?' he checked as she neared her peak, but Maggie could not answer. Instead, her fingers did, for they pressed into his hair in a plea for more of the same.

He did not relent, not even as she came—he kept probing as she arched and the sensation was so intense, so consuming, that she only recalled her name when he said it.

'Maggie.'

It was neither a summons nor a question; he just rested a second on his heels and watched her pleasurable spasms.

She lay as if stunned, barely moving as he leant over her. Ilyas flipped open a small wooden box, and she lay watching and silent as he sheathed himself.

She would never regret this, Maggie knew.

He rose over her and positioned himself with precision. Her legs felt heavy from her deep climax, so he parted them with his and then leant up on his forearms. Ilyas's face was over hers and she looked at his mouth and wondered how she tasted.

'Delicious,' he said, as if he knew her question. He licked his lips, tasting her again, and she stirred back to sensual life beneath him. But her recovery was not complete, for she was still breathless and her sex felt raw. Somehow, she was still ruled by desire and she ached for that kiss.

He did not deliver one.

Even though her hands coiled behind his neck, he refused to lower his mouth and she thought she would die from longing.

Instead, she felt the nudge of him at her entrance and she stared into his eyes. He watched her closely as he pressed a little further in.

And he kept on watching as she squeezed her eyes closed, for there was no denying it hurt. But then, when she gathered her breath, when this time her hips rose to welcome his when he entered just a little, she opened her eyes and he drove in.

Maggie cried out, but he covered her mouth with his and swallowed her pain.

Of course it hurt; he was large and she was untouched, and no amount of tenderness could have negated that. And there were stars, though not the kind she had hoped to see as he drove in deeply. His arm slipped beneath the small of her back, lifting her to him as he took her slowly again.

His mouth moved from Maggie's and came by her temple where he tasted the salt of a tear.

She did not cry and she was not now, not really. And soon they were kissing again, and her body rose to urge him to move faster to keep pace with her desire for a more punishing rhythm.

But it was Ilyas now who refused to be rushed.

He liked the feel of her unfurling to his touch and the tight grip of her as he took her at his leisure. And he liked their brief kisses when their mouths sometimes met, and the feel of her hands on his torso.

His body was hard and muscled beneath her fingers; even the flesh of his buttocks was taut as he demanded more and more of her body.

Maggie gripped his legs with hers as her internal muscles clenched and he unleashed the full force of his passion. He held her arms over her head and increased the pace, taking her fast now.

The sole of her foot pushed against the back of his thigh and she felt as if she were climbing him as her body was energised by his power. The shout that heralded his release was primal and as he spilled himself inside her, Maggie came hard. Each nerve felt like it was brushed with live wires.

It had hurt, yes.

But it had been the most beautiful pain she had ever known. Maggie lay there with his weight atop her, the sounds of the *quanoon* returning to her ears.

She had never wanted anyone like this before.

For years she had wondered if there was something missing in her, something wrong even, for she had never really been attracted to anyone before, and had never known true desire.

Until Ilyas.

CHAPTER EIGHT

ONE NIGHT IN his bed.

Even as she entered the vast sleeping area, Maggie knew that was all she would have.

Maggie knew her hair was tousled and did not want to hazard a guess as to what she looked like. As he had helped her to stand up, she had seen the smears of blood on her thighs from the rough coupling. Her face felt raw from his kisses and her hair, when she had ran her fingers through it, was knotted.

But she had never felt better in her life.

Always she covered herself—never emerging, even from the shower, anything other than fully dressed. Yet she walked naked with him and barely gave it a thought.

The area was terribly male. While her bed in the desert abode was dressed in silk and pretty cushions, his was adorned with heavy furs.

'I should protest really,' she said as he draped one over her.

'Have you any idea how cold it gets at night here in winter?'

'No,' Maggie said and shivered, not just at the cool air but at the thought that she would never know.

'Don't you have a fire in here?' Maggie asked, simply

wanting to know everything she could and surprised at the rare absence of anything in these very luxurious surroundings, for it was cold in here!

'Not in the bedroom,' he said, and slid under the fur, pulling her in beside him. 'Here is for sleeping.'

'And sex,' Maggie said, and she looked up at a rope that hung over the bed.

'Of course.'

'Do you have a harem in the desert too?' she asked, loathing the thought, yet unbearably curious.

'The women of the *hammam* take it in turns to come out here.'

'A holiday to the desert?' she said. 'That was sarcasm—'

'I know it was,' Ilyas interrupted, 'but you are correct. They enjoy coming out here. It is more…' He stopped.

'More what?'

Never, not once, not even for a fleeting moment had he protected a lover from the truth of his lifestyle, yet he hesitated now.

'More what?' Maggie persisted.

'I have more time for them when I am here.'

Ouch!

It was like stabbing pins into her eyes, yet she sought the truth no matter how it hurt to hear it. 'What about when you go away?' Maggie asked. 'Do they travel with you?'

'A select few.'

They lay on their sides facing each other, absolutely together yet their lives were worlds apart.

He had her heart. Even if she had never had feelings like this before, already Maggie knew it.

She also knew that Ilyas had no heart to give.

'What happens when you marry?' she asked.

'My harem gets disbanded.'

'*Your* harem?'

'Of course.'

Ilyas took care of his harem and certainly they only took care of him. The uncomfortable thought of her with his brother resurfaced then. There was a feeling unknown, that burnt at his very core, but it was a feeling he could not name.

For he had never been jealous in his lifetime.

Ilyas had never been driven by the need to possess, for, in general, whatever he wanted he claimed with ease.

Except for the title of king.

But it was not jealousy he felt there, it was more anger about his father's ways.

He looked at Maggie and tried to explain how his life ran, when he had never cared to explain it before.

'I must be faithful to my wife.'

'Must?' Maggie frowned. 'You make it sound like a chore.'

'A future king should not marry for love,' Ilyas said. 'In fact, it is frowned upon.'

And as Maggie lay there, bristling with indignation, she recalled the tales told around the fire as Ilyas explained further.

'We are taught that to marry for love creates a weakness. If you and I were to…' Again he hesitated, for that was not the example he wanted to give; it revealed that there were feelings. Even as he reluctantly acknowledged their existence, out loud he corrected himself. 'If there is love, what if that person was taken?'

Maggie stared as he spoke.

'What might a king relinquish in order to secure her return?' He waited, but Maggie did not answer. 'Marriage is a means to provide an heir.'

'Charming.'

'I didn't make the rules,' Ilyas said. 'Your friend Suzanne does not understand who she deals with. My father would cut Hazin off rather than pay her a single cent.'

'She's not my friend,' Maggie said, and rolled onto her back and stared up at the billowing ceiling.

She loathed his cold world.

But not him.

'What about Hazin?' Maggie asked, thinking back to the time she had spent with his brother and what he had told her. 'Are the rules the same for him?'

'He was not born to be king,' Ilyas answered. 'And he knows and abuses that fact with appalling regularity.'

'You do love your brother.' Maggie smiled for though he spoke with derision she could hear the veiled affection. 'After all, you are fighting to cover for him.'

'Leave it,' Ilyas warned.

The harem he could speak about, but the subject of his brother he closed. Ilyas pulled her back to his arms and they lay looking up at the ceiling that wasn't so billowing now, and both could hear that the winds were starting to die down.

'Is it morning?' Maggie asked.

'Not yet,' he told her. 'But it will be soon—sunrise is almost here.'

'This time tomorrow I'll be getting ready to go to the airport,' Maggie said. 'Assuming you let me leave.'

'I shall inform the palace to send a helicopter at midday and you can return to your hostel.'

She would make her flight, Maggie realised, only now she wasn't so sure that she wanted to. Instead, she wanted the simoom to pick up again, to be lost in his world for just a little while longer, for it was bliss to lie here, being held in his arms.

'How do you feel about going home?'

And unlike when Suzanne or others had asked the inevitable question, he waited for her to gather her thoughts before responding.

'Tired,' Maggie admitted. 'I feel wonderful after such an extended holiday and I'm all relaxed, but when I think about going home…' She thought some more. 'As much as I'm looking forward to seeing everyone, I'm tired at the thought of starting over again.'

'In what way?'

'Well, I'll stay on Flo's sofa while I find somewhere to live. She has a tiny flat so it will only be temporary. I'd love my own place but I can't see that ever happening so it will mean finding a flat-share and then getting to know new flatmates…'

'Like when you are travelling?'

Maggie thought about it for a moment and then nodded. 'It actually feels a lot like that, but without the fun of a holiday.'

'Who raised you after your mother died?'

'I had a lot of temporary carers. Some were for longer than others. It's harder to place older children,' she explained. 'I was with a couple of families for long-term placements but they didn't work out.'

'Why didn't they work out?'

Maggie stretched and went to get up—she really didn't like to dwell on those days—but he pulled her back in so she rested on his chest and he asked the question again.

Usually he asked no questions in the bedroom, but for some reason he was curious about Maggie.

'The first was a year or so after my mother died. I was there for a few months, but then the marriage broke up and they…' She gave a tense shrug. 'I doubt, with their marriage crumbling, that access to me was high on their priorities.'

'And the other home?'

Maggie never spoke of it and she wasn't sure that she was ready to now.

Even Flo didn't know, and they discussed most things. Maggie tended to gloss over that time.

It simply hurt too much to go into detail, even in her own thoughts.

His arm was holding her, though; her head was on his chest and he was stroking her hair. There was patience in the air and she wondered if now she could share it.

'I had just started high school. I lived in a care home and was doing okay when I was told that there was a possible family interested in a long-term placement, possibly adoption.'

'When you say "doing okay", what do you mean?'

'I was happy enough,' Maggie said. 'I liked my new school and the carers were nice and, since I'd lost my mother, it was probably the most stable time I'd known. Anyway, this family seemed nice. They had three sons and I used to go there some weekends and then for longer on holidays.' Maggie thought back. 'It felt like I was on trial. Diane wanted a daughter and that was going to be me. She wanted someone who was going to go and get her nails done with her and go clothes shopping and things. Well, we went shopping and she said she couldn't wait till the holidays and we'd go to the movies…'

Maggie fell silent as she gathered her thoughts and she liked it that he didn't push her to speak.

'I've never liked the movies.' She admitted what she hadn't been able to tell Diane at the time. 'But I went. And she made all the big promises…'

'Like?'

'Like, when I moved in I could decorate my bedroom how I wanted to and that we'd get a puppy.'

'Did she follow through?'

'Oh, yes.' Maggie nodded. 'I moved in and we did up the bedroom and then we went and chose him. A little Scottie dog and we called him Patch. I started my new school…'

'Another new school?' he checked, and Maggie nodded.

'How was life then?'

Ilyas could not guess or know, yet he wanted to hear it exactly.

'Hard,' Maggie said, and there was a note of anguish as she re-examined that time. 'It was a new school, new family, new everything, and I was trying to fit in with them all. She started me at ballet…'

'And we both know you can't dance!'

He made her smile.

In the midst of the hardest part, he made her smile just a bit, but even the little joke was telling. He already knew her better than Diane ever had.

'Apparently I wasn't grateful enough. And I wasn't happy enough for her liking. She was upset that I didn't call her Mum, but as I said to the case-worker, even if she was dead, I already had one. Maybe I should have just called her what she wanted, maybe in time I would have, but Diane decided I was too much trouble.'

It was actually right to examine that time, Maggie realised. For years it had been too hard to, but lying in Ilyas's arms made it doable.

'I wasn't trouble,' she told Ilyas. 'Believe me, I've seen trouble, and I was nowhere near that. I like my own space, I like to read, but Diane wanted entertainment on demand and a playmate...'

'She wanted a living doll?' Ilyas offered, and Maggie hesitated.

She had never thought of it like that, but it had felt *exactly* that.

'Yes!' She nodded, so glad that he understood—that he had voiced what she hadn't been able to articulate, even to herself. 'But I wasn't the daughter she'd envisaged and so she labelled me as trouble. I came home from school one day and there was a social worker waiting and I was told that things hadn't worked out.'

'You were taken back to the care home?'

'No, they were full,' Maggie said. 'So I was placed in another.'

It had been time to start over again.

'What about the dog?' he asked. 'Patch?'

And she gave a thin smile because it was a little odd to hear him ask fondly about something like that.

But then her smile died. 'She got rid of him too,' Maggie said bitterly. 'No doubt he was also too much trouble.'

She peeled herself from his embrace and sat up and he watched as she picked at the fur rug. He noted that she didn't cry and he wondered if she had at the time.

But, then, who would have comforted her?

It was disconcerting the emotion that swept through him as he lay there, because usually he did not allow for such things.

A tender heart was not a part of his job description, yet he sat up and put a hand on her shoulder, pulling her in, and Maggie let herself be held.

'I hate her so much,' Maggie admitted. 'I know it's not healthy to, but I hate what she did.'

'So do I,' Ilyas agreed.

'Your brother's lucky to have you,' Maggie said. 'I was jealous before when I said you were wrong to be so protective of him… I always wanted that, someone who loved me enough to look out for me. The carers were good and everything but it's not the same as family…'

'When did you leave the home?'

'I had weekend work with Paul at the café. When I was sixteen and I went into semi-independent lodgings he took me on full time. I've been there since…'

'Eating chocolate.'

She was grateful that he sensed she was through talking about it and ended it for her with a smile.

'Yes.'

It was close to sunrise.

He heard the bells as the maid approached and they both lay silent as she placed refreshments by the bed.

'I have to get up,' he told her.

Maggie loathed this morning.

He climbed out of bed and took a drink, and Maggie watched as he pulled on a robe and belted it. She said nothing.

Neither did Ilyas.

He walked through the corridors and stepped outside the desert abode.

The wind had dropped, but there was the chaos it had left in its wake and he looked over to where some of the smaller tents had collapsed; one of the workers was rounding up some horses that had run loose. Ilyas could only imagine the chaos back in the city.

He wanted to return to bed—for the first time in his life, he wanted to turn his back on the many things that needed to be done. But he had been raised with duty as his priority. First he prayed, and then he made contact with the palace to find out how his people had fared during the nights he had been gone.

'You are needed back here,' Mahmoud informed him. 'There is a lot of damage and there are people missing.'

And that could not wait for midday.

He spoke with Mahmoud for several moments about all that was going on and then he asked another question.

'Have you spoken with Hazin about the threats?' Ilyas asked. He believed now that nothing had gone on.

So certain was Ilyas that there were no tapes, the question was almost an afterthought.

'I have,' Mahmoud said.

'And?' Ilyas checked, anxious to get back to Maggie, and to spend together the little time alone that they had before the helicopter came.

'He has asked that we submit to their demands.'

'Hazin said that?' Ilyas fought to keep his voice and breathing even, yet he could hear the blood pulsing in his ears at Mahmoud's unexpected response—he had been certain, *certain* that there were no tapes. 'What exactly did he say?'

But Mahmoud pointed out that it should not be discussed over the phone. 'It would be better if we speak face to face.'

As Ilyas prayed, Maggie headed back to her own area to wash. She smiled at the maiden who was waiting for her when she came out.

There was a pale lilac robe on the bed and the maiden coiled and loosely tied Maggie's hair.

'Thank you,' Maggie said, but as the maiden went to help her dress Maggie declined.

Once alone, though, Maggie struggled with the tiny buttons at the back, but finally she had it on and stood and looked at her reflection in the huge mirror. For such a sleepless night she looked well groomed. She tried to fathom all that had happened.

Not so much the sex, more all that she had told him. All they had shared.

Maggie heard the sound of bells and knew from the footsteps that it was him.

She didn't turn around; somehow she knew he bore bad news and she stood looking in the mirror as he came and stood behind her.

'The helicopter is being sent for us now,' he told her.

'I thought we had the morning.'

'There is a lot of damage from the simoom.'

She should feel guilty for being so shallow, Maggie thought, but her head was too full of them to allow room for other emotions.

Perhaps his ways were the right ways, Maggie pondered, because she could barely contemplate packing her clothes, let alone attempting to run a country when her mind was so mired by them.

'I can't imagine being back at the hostel,' she admitted as she turned around and faced him.

'You shan't be going back there,' Ilyas said, but his voice came out too harsh. 'I am taking you back to the palace with me. But first we need to speak about what went on between you and Hazin.'

'Are you saying you still don't believe me?' She frowned at his narrowed gaze. 'Do you still think there's a tape that might come out?'

'You are to tell me what went on.'

'Ilyas?' She felt her temper building. 'I didn't sleep with your brother, or do you think it was fake blood on my thigh…?'

'Clearly you didn't sleep with him,' Ilyas snapped, and then he reminded himself of his status. He was not about to let his judgement be clouded just because he had slept with her. 'But that does not get you off the hook—there are other ways to give pleasure, and I would expect them to send a virgin to lure him…'

She went to slap him.

Maggie did not condone violence, not in any way, shape or form, but neither would she stand there while the man who had taken her virginity practically called her a whore.

He caught her hand.

'I really wouldn't recommend slapping the crown prince,' he warned as his fingers tightened around her wrist and halted her hand's angry progression.

So she slapped him with her free hand instead.

He didn't even flinch. If anything, it was Maggie who flinched at the sound of her hand hitting his flesh.

'You want to play that game?' Ilyas checked.

'No…' she answered, suddenly nervous.

'Then know this—if you *ever* slap me again, I shall put you straight over my knee and show you how it's done properly! I shall return the favour so hard that you will be asking for an ice bucket to sit on for the flight home.'

His words hit home, for at the reminder she would be leaving her features moved from defiant to crestfallen, but he misinterpreted the change.

'I'm not going to hurt you,' Ilyas said, and dropped her wrist. 'Maggie, what happened in that cabin? What is it you cannot tell me?'

Hell, yes, it mattered.

Not just that she might have been sent there to lure his brother, and not even for what might have taken place.

It mattered now because Ilyas cared more than he should for Maggie, and he knew now that it was jealousy that tore up his chest.

'We were talking,' Maggie said, and gave an uncomfortable shrug. 'About feelings.'

'That cannot be right. Hazin doesn't talk about such things…'

'Perhaps not to an emotional desert like you!' Maggie shouted.

He didn't match her tone, but his voice was low and ominous in return. 'What was he saying?' Ilyas demanded, for he could not stand not knowing a second longer. 'Maggie, game over, you are to tell me, so whatever it is, whatever has happened, I can best deal with it.'

'I told him I was low about my mother. That it was the anniversary of her death and he opened up…'

'Please.' Ilyas shook his head, wondering even now

if her story about her childhood was true. Perhaps she had been angling to get his brother to provide a shoulder to cry on as a way to seduce him? Ilyas knew for a fact it would never have worked and he told her why. 'My brother does not bend to sob stories.'

'No, he doesn't!' Maggie flared. 'He's rather refreshing, in fact. He told me I was better off without family.' She was through covering for the al-Razims, or for anyone else for that matter. 'He said he hopes his father does disinherit him…'

Ilyas fell silent as he suddenly realised why Hazin would not want the tapes to get out, but Maggie had not finished turning the knife.

'And it wasn't a sob story I gave him,' she cried. 'I was just saying that it was a hard day and he got it, he said that he loathed anniversaries…'

'Enough!' Ilyas shouted.

He had demanded that she tell him, insisted upon the truth, but now that she came close to revealing all, suddenly he did not want to hear it.

'Get ready,' he told her, 'the chopper will soon be here.'

But Maggie was no longer silent and as he went to stride off she caught at his robe.

'He told me that he got it,' she said, and Ilyas turned.

She watched as his features turned to granite, as the swarthy skin paled to milk as she voiced what others, even Ilyas, could not speak of.

'Hazin told me about his wife!'

CHAPTER NINE

THE FACT THAT Hazin had spoken to Maggie about his late wife stunned Ilyas.

'I don't…' His voice trailed off, when it was rare he wavered.

Ilyas had been about to say that he didn't believe Maggie, but he didn't finish his sentence.

It was clear she was speaking the truth, yet it truly confused him for the brother he knew never spoke about feelings and certainly not about his wife.

Ever.

Petra's death had been the tragedy that had befallen the palace all those years ago but it had been rarely spoken of since.

And while Ilyas was fighting to keep his brother from being disinherited, from what Maggie had just said, Hazin was actively fighting to lose his title.

'He spoke to you about Petra?'

Maggie nodded.

'What did he say?'

'He told me that she died nearly ten years ago.' She cast her mind back to the conversation. 'He said there is a new wing at the hospital, due to be opened in her name, and he's supposed to deliver a speech. He doesn't want to…'

'What else?'

'Ilyas.' Maggie shook her head. 'I'm not going to relay everything that we discussed.'

'I'm asking you to.'

'No!' Maggie shook her head. 'We're not partners, you've made that abundantly clear, yet you expect me to open up to you completely and to betray Hazin's trust.'

'Your conversation with my brother was clearly an intimate one.'

'Yes, but it didn't take place on a pillow.'

She wanted that with him instead.

And Ilyas wanted the same.

'We're lovers,' he said. 'You can tell me.'

'We *were* lovers,' Maggie corrected. 'Once.'

'Come on, Maggie.' His voice showed a rare glimpse of the disquiet he felt on that matter. 'We both know it felt like more than a one-night stand.'

It was cruel of him to play that card, Maggie thought. Cruel of him to push for whispers and private conversations to take place now when, by his own rules, it could be nothing more than sex, no matter what he said about how it had felt.

'If being lovers for one night gives you carte blanche access to me, then I deserve the same from you. So tell me, Ilyas, why, if it felt like more than a one-night stand, would you let me simply walk away?'

He looked at her and for one dangerous moment considered telling Maggie the real reason they could never be.

The real reason that he chose not to pursue a relationship or marry.

But he didn't.

Ilyas had learned long ago to tell no one of the plans he had made.

Not the elders or his trusted advisors. Not even his brother, who was next in line to the throne.

It was safer that way.

Certainly he would not be telling a woman he had met just a short while ago.

A woman who could be involved in a threat to the monarchy.

It was easier to believe she might still be responsible, better to think that she might be a threat, because it meant he could more readily keep her at arm's length.

'But I'm not letting you walk away,' he told Maggie. 'You shall return to the palace with me. I want to speak with Mahmoud and Hazin before I set you free.'

His words doused her like ice. 'You just did.'

He frowned. 'I don't understand what you mean.'

'You just did set me free, Ilyas. For a little while there I forgot that I was your prisoner, but thanks for reminding me of that fact.'

Making love with him and then lying in bed and talking like lovers while being held in his arms, Maggie had managed to push from her mind the method by which she had arrived there.

Not anymore.

'I shan't be forgetting again.'

Regardless of the means by which she had arrived, it was still hard for her to leave.

Maggie took one last look at the bedded area where she had spent those first, frightening hours and remembered him forcing her to take a drink.

She stepped out to the living area where they had made love.

Now, though, there was anger in the air and it hurt to leave this way.

'We have to go now.'

Ilyas strode past her and out to the waiting area. Maggie remembered the maidens' attempts at kindness so she went and thanked them, though Maggie wasn't sure that they understood in the least what she said.

She and Ilyas sat in silence on the flight back to the palace.

Maggie stared out of the window and wished the desert would never end, but of course it did. The sparse trees became more frequent and then a building appeared and she could see the horses in their fields.

Then another building, and another.

She looked over at Ilyas and wished he would order the helicopter to turn around. Instead, their eyes met and he stared back at her.

He tried to fathom her. She was, quite simply, the most complex woman he had met. The most complex person.

She spoke with both maidens and grieving princes. She danced when she could not. She laughed but never cried, despite the weight of sadness on her shoulders. There was that one tear he had tasted… He couldn't help remembering the bliss of that time.

Ilyas had never craved closeness. But he had found himself telling Maggie things he usually would not consider revealing.

And for Ilyas that was the most troublesome part of it all.

He had plans in place that not another soul knew, and yet here he sat considering sharing them with her.

No!

He shifted his gaze to a safer place than the green pools of her eyes and looked down at a red line of canyons that indicated they were approaching the palace.

This spectacular air approach was lost to Maggie as she continued to stare at his profile. Those cheeks had once been next to hers while locked in bliss, that mouth she had caressed with her own was set now in a grim line and his features were stern.

'Ilyas…' she said.

He ignored her.

'Ilyas?'

'We're here.'

He disembarked first and was greeted with a salute. He strode ahead fast and Maggie had to almost run to keep up with him.

The palace grounds were confusing and there wasn't a moment to get her bearings, she just followed him onto an ornate bridge and at the other end a door was held open.

Ilyas looked around, impatient for staff to arrive, for he wanted Maggie safely out of sight.

Her desire for conversation was apparent and he dared not indulge her.

'I need to get on,' he told her. 'Someone will be here to take care of you soon.'

'You're just going to leave me here?'

'Do you expect to stand holding hands?'

'I expect manners,' Maggie said.

Damn you, impossible woman! Manners were the last thing on his mind.

He did not deal with emotion, yet it coursed through

him now. He wanted to kiss that temper out of her, he wanted to take her this very moment to his bed.

But there was a country to run.

He turned to the sound of footsteps and Maggie watched as a tall woman approached. She wore her long dark hair up and looked terribly official.

And cross!

She said something in Arabic that Maggie guessed was a request to know who she was, for Ilyas answered the woman with her name.

'Maggie Delaney,' he responded, and then a rather lengthy conversation in Arabic ensued, or rather the woman spoke angrily for a couple of moments before Ilyas interrupted her.

'Maggie is a guest of the palace.'

He spoke in English and must have asked her to do the same because she turned and looked down her nose at Maggie and then gave a shrug, though she did, albeit reluctantly, switch to English.

Perhaps it would have been better if she had not.

'Well, your guest will just have to amuse herself,' the woman said rudely, and then looked back at Ilyas. 'You need to meet with the king. Now.'

The woman walked off and Maggie stood there.

'Are all your staff so pleasant?' Maggie enquired. Given she had been dragged from her bed by his henchmen, she felt her question was merited.

'That was my mother, the queen.'

Oh, dear!

'Your mother?'

Maggie had honestly thought it was an annoyed PA or an aggrieved assistant. She had spoken to her son with as much warmth as she had greeted Maggie.

And then Maggie looked at Ilyas and responded to the way she had been introduced by him.

'I'm not a guest,' she reminded him. 'I believe I'm being held against my will.'

'No,' he said, and now, when finally their eyes met, the anger within him died on the spot. 'You are my guest.'

'So you believe that nothing happened between Hazin and me other than talking?'

He said nothing.

Yes, he believed her, but it actually didn't matter what had taken place, Ilyas thought.

There was nothing Hazin had said or done that could prove a bigger threat to the monarchy than the woman who stood before him now.

His plans had been a lifetime in the making and she threatened them now merely by her presence.

He suddenly understood a little better his brother wanting to be disinherited, for at that very moment Ilyas could have gladly walked away from it all too.

But duty was ingrained in him so deeply that it would take more than a feeling to make him walk away.

'I have to work,' he told her.

Although they were speaking, Maggie wanted the luxury of time—time to hammer things out and then sulk for a suitable while.

And time to make up!

There was none, though.

'I really do have to go,' he said. 'Apparently some tourists were trapped in the desert by the simoom. It has caused quite an international incident.'

'Oh, no!'

'Oh, yes, and it was actually your tour operator

who ran into problems. The rest heeded advice and cancelled.'

'Was anybody hurt?'

'No, they were able to take shelter and ride it out. For now, they have all been transferred to a hotel where the press are gathered. It would seem they were without food and there was only limited water.' He looked at her as they *both* remembered the morning Maggie had arrived in his desert abode and he had insisted that she drink. 'You had rather a lucky escape after all...'

'I'm not so sure about that,' Maggie said, attempting indignation. But then she looked at the man she had spent the most memorable time of her life with, and *that* was coming off a year of adventure.

But their time was almost over.

And she was still cross at all he had insinuated.

So very cross.

Yet, overriding all that, Maggie was more daunted by the finality that was looming up on them.

'Shall I see you again?' she asked.

'No.'

She looked at his cheek where she had slapped him, though of course there was no evidence of it.

She had left no mark.

Not even, she guessed, on his heart.

But then he relented.

'I will come and say farewell in the morning,' Ilyas said. 'I am going to be very busy today. I shall be working until well after midnight.'

Then, as if to prove how busy he was, a very distinguished-looking gentleman approached. 'Your Highness.'

He was far more polite than the queen had been,

and when he saw Maggie he spoke in English. He introduced himself as Mahmoud, the king's advisor, and then he turned to Ilyas and explained that the king was considering speaking with some leaders and diplomats about the tourists. 'I really think it would be beneficial if you were the one to reach out…'

'Of course,' Ilyas responded. 'Could you give me a moment, Mahmoud?'

The man bowed and then backed off.

'You shall be looked after,' Ilyas said. 'You have been given a suite in the west wing and I have asked that Kumu take care of you. She speaks English. If you would prefer to return to the hostel, though, I completely understand…'

'I'm free to leave?' she checked.

It would be so much easier on him if she did.

So much easier on Ilyas for Maggie to storm out now and never look back.

'Yes,' he said. 'You are free to go.'

'Well, in that case…' Maggie smiled, glad to have the choice to leave and the luxury of the choice to remain. 'I might just hang around.'

Damn.

Kumu was warm and friendly as she showed Maggie to her suite. It was quite simply stunning, with a formal lounge area and then a large bedroom with French windows that opened up to a balcony that had a view of the desert from which she had just come.

Nothing was too much trouble.

In fact, her belongings had been brought over from the hostel and had all been beautifully laundered. Her clothes, which had seen better days thanks to living out of a backpack, were now all pressed and hanging up. 'I shall pack for you this evening,' Kumu said. 'Would you like to wear a robe to fly home in?'

Maggie was about to decline but then Kumu added, 'His Royal Highness shall be coming to say farewell in the morning.'

'A robe would be lovely,' Maggie agreed.

She was actually thrilled to know that she would have a little keepsake to remind her of her time here.

Left alone, she removed her jewelled slippers and was about to walk out to the balcony and tip out the sand when she halted.

Maggie went through her backpack and found an old envelope where she had collected menus and tickets and such things.

She pulled them out and then took off her slippers, tipping the small bit of sand into the paper, even gathering a little that she spilled from it on the floor. Then she licked the envelope and sealed within it her tiny memento of the desert.

Of course, she needed no real reminders.

How could she ever forget?

If ever there was a perfect end to a holiday then Maggie knew she had found it.

After a light lunch she was given an insider's tour of the palace. Maggie had seen it from the plane and its outline from the desert, but nothing could have prepared her for its internal beauty.

The palace was its own mini city, Kumu explained as she took her through stunning gardens, lush with flowers and water displays, and into a very modern compound. There were offices and kitchens, though there were separate ones for the workers and royals. 'And guests.' Kumu smiled. 'You shall select from the same menu as the queen tonight.'

'Do the royals come to this part?' Maggie asked, hoping for a glimpse of Ilyas, but Kumu shook her head.

'Not really.'

They left the compound and Maggie was led to the ornate bridge she had walked across with Ilyas. But whereas Ilyas had strode ahead, Kumu took her time.

'From here you can see the royal jets.' Kumu pointed. 'The palace has its own runway and there is the landing pad where we just came from. Here is where you might see a royal returning from a function or overseas trip.'

'And I thought they just sat around eating grapes,' Maggie said, and then worried that her humour might be misconstrued as rude, but Kumu laughed.

'Oh, there is plenty of that too. Come, I will show you the main entrance where dignitaries are greeted.'

It too was amazing.

The huge display of flowers, on closer inspection, turned out to be jewels. And the hummingbirds that drank the nectar were gold encrusted with rubies and emeralds.

She could gaze upon that display alone for hours, yet there was still so much to see. There were huge marble pillars and the ceiling was so high Maggie had to extend her head back fully to see it; she stood like that for several moments utterly in awe. It was as if Michelangelo had spent half his lifetime right here in Zayrinia, for the artwork on the ceiling was breathtaking.

'Come and see the portraits,' Kumu said, and Maggie found herself looking up at a huge portrait of a very forbidding-looking man and his wife.

The queen was younger in the portrait than the woman Maggie had seen briefly, but though very beautiful there was still a coldness to her eyes.

There was another painting of them with their children. Ilyas must have been about eleven or twelve, Maggie guessed, but he had been an old head on young shoulders even then. She looked right into the beautifully captured intense hazel eyes and then smiled at his serious expression.

Of course it was not returned!

The surprise, though, was Hazin, for she had expected a cheeky smile or a glimpse of the wild prince to come but, no, he stood rigid and formal, and as impeccably groomed as his older brother.

And then Maggie's throat seemed to close a little, for the next portrait was of a very young Hazin and his bride.

'She was beautiful,' Maggie said.

'And kind.' Kumu sighed. 'She always had a smile for me and said thank you...' Maggie glanced sideways and saw that there were actually tears in Kumu's eyes.

Maggie guessed that smiles and kind words were somewhat missing here.

'Princess Petra was so happy on her wedding day,' Kumu said as she gazed at the young bride. 'She loved Hazin so very much.'

They moved along, even if Maggie would have loved to linger and find out more.

It wasn't her place to, though.

Oh, how could she bear to leave? Maggie thought, for the palace and its many secrets had won her heart too.

'And here is our future king.' Kumu's voice was proud as she introduced a formal portrait of Ilyas. Maggie felt her throat tighten as she saw a side to Ilyas she had never seen before. On his arm was a falcon and he was dressed like a warrior. 'Here the crown prince wears the traditional attire of the al-Razims yet the setting is less formal, for he loves the desert and is a skilled falconer.'

No matter what they had shared in the desert, there was so much that she didn't know about him, Maggie thought.

He was dressed in black, as he had been on the night they had met, but unlike then there was a heavy sword to his side and the *kafeyah* was black and tied with a silver cord. Maggie had known he was imposing; there had been no doubt the night they had met. But perhaps now, for the first time, Maggie truly understood just how unattainable he was.

He would be king.

She would have stared at the painting for hours if she could. Soon Maggie was shown the ancient stone benches where the forefathers had first sat as they'd met to discuss the running of this beautiful land.

'And there is a *hammam* beneath?' Maggie asked, carefully avoiding the real question, for she was desperate to hear about the harem!

'Oh, yes, the *hammam* is stunning.' Kumu nodded. 'You shall go there this afternoon.'

'Really?'

'Of course. All our guests love to visit the *hammam*—it is the highlight of their trip!' Kumu said as she walked Maggie back to her suite. 'There you can unwind and be pampered in preparation for your journey home. I shall come and collect you around four if that is suitable for you?'

Oh, yes!

* * *

Maggie had been told to just wear the *hammam* towel that had been left out for her, but being Maggie she also put on her bikini and still felt way too exposed.

'Shouldn't I cover up a bit more?' Maggie checked when Kumu came to collect her.

'Why?' Kumu frowned and then let out a giggle. 'You shall not be walking through the palace! Here…' She opened a door that Maggie had assumed led to a wardrobe, but instead there were steps. 'You are in the west wing so you have your own access,' Kumu explained, with another giggle at the thought of her walking half-naked through the palace. 'The *hammam* is for women.'

'I see,' Maggie said, though she didn't, for Ilyas had told her he was a frequent visitor there and Kumu had said that all the guests loved it.

She guessed the men's and women's areas were kept separate and no doubt the royals had an area of their own, as they did in the palace.

They exited the stairs and Maggie was led through a maze of candlelit corridors, lined with intricate tiles that she could just make out were the darkest blue.

It felt like night.

Maggie entered an area where several women awaited. They were all dressed in cream-coloured robes and Kumu explained that the maidens were here to take care of her.

'Just me?'

'Just you.' Kumu smiled. 'Enjoy.'

It was oddly freeing that there were no others.

And though the maidens laughed as she clung onto her bikini, they were not unkind about it and finally Maggie stripped off and lay down.

She felt horribly awkward at first, yet the women chatted with each other as they scrubbed her with salt. Sometimes they practised a little English and asked if she was okay.

Gradually Maggie was.

The *hammam* worked its magic and she lay there with her eyes closed and thought about the tales told around the campfire and could scarcely believe she was actually here, in a part of Zayrinia few knew existed.

Her hair and scalp were massaged with oil and she found out that *halawa* was sort of like being waxed, except they were exceptionally skilled at it, compared to Maggie's occasional poor efforts.

She was exfoliated and tidied to within an inch of her life, and even her eyebrows were threaded.

After her skin had been scrubbed from head to toe she was led to a small area and told to rinse off beneath a stream of water.

It was neither cool nor warm and Maggie stood there for ages, relishing the luxurious experience. But as she made her way back she became a little lost. All the tunnels looked the same and then she entered one that was not familiar, for the tiles were no longer blue. Instead they were a dark crimson and the patterns were more delicate.

She had thought she was in heaven before but this was truly paradise.

The candles were fragrant and the air was richly scented. As she looked at the tiles she saw that, unlike where she had come from, these weren't patterned; they were, in fact, murals.

And they were stunning. Then, as she narrowed her eyes to see them better, Maggie felt her newly scrubbed skin flush, for they depicted scenes that she had never even imagined—dozens of beautiful, naked, long-haired women and just one man!

Maggie tore her eyes away from the images and saw that there were little fonts built into walls. When she dipped her fingers in, Maggie found they were filled with oil.

She inhaled the sensual fragrance on her fingers and found that she was drawn to look at the images again. Suddenly, from behind her, she heard a burst of laughter. Looking down the candlelit tunnel, she saw a glow of soft light and guessed that the end of this passage housed the harem.

She looked up and, sure enough, she could see a thick velvet rope, like the one in the desert, and she could see the now familiar stream of bells that lined the passageway.

Maggie turned and fled, back to the gorgeous blue tiles where she ran into one of the maidens, who looked troubled when she saw where Maggie had come from.

'La, la!' the maiden called, telling her, no, she must not go there. 'Not for you,' she scolded, wagging her finger.

'I got lost,' Maggie said, and, blushing, she apologised as she was led to a seat.

There she had her nails painted the most gorgeous shade of coral. The maidens were really laughing and chatting and Maggie knew it was about her little detour.

She even joined in.

'I took a wrong turn!'

'There are things you should never see!' The maiden smiled now.

And then, after hours of being pampered, her wonderful spa was over.

Oh, she could happily live like this for ever, Maggie thought as she was taken back to her suite by Kumu.

Kumu told her she was married and had a daughter and that her husband worked in the palace too.

'Do you like working here?'

It was, Maggie had first assumed, a natural question, but even as it left her lips she realised she had crossed a line as Kumu tensed and paused before answering carefully.

'Of course,' Kumu responded stiffly. 'I love to work.'

It was an evasive response to a question that Maggie should not have asked, and she could have kicked herself for her insensitivity—for of course Kumu was in no position to answer honestly.

It was actually a relief when there was a knock on the door and a light supper was wheeled in.

'I shall leave you now,' Kumu said. 'You shall sleep well after your time in the *hammam*, and I shall come and wake you up early so that you can be at the airport in plenty of time for your flight. I shall do your hair…'

'I don't need to have my hair done to fly.'

But Kumu was insistent.

'Thank you,' Maggie said as Kumu headed for the door. 'It really has been a wonderful day.'

It had been and Kumu was right, she was tired from the *hammam*, but, having eaten her supper, when there was nothing for Maggie to do but rest, she found that she could not.

She went out onto the balcony and watched the most stunning sunset—a massive ball of orange swallowed by the fiery sands. Finally, stars were emerging in the Zayrinian sky.

Not just stars but, as the night sky darkened, constellations and even a galaxy emerged—a misty swirl of mossy green, gold and lilacs.

There was barely a breath of wind, and the desert looked so still as the sky moved above it. Even though it grew cold, she did not care.

She would never see the sky like this again, Maggie knew.

Even if she returned some time in the future, even if she could afford the very best tour, she would never stand on a balcony as if on the edge of the world, bathed in the light of a trillion stars.

And, after their brief farewell tomorrow, she would never see *him* again.

Maggie loathed that they had ended on a row.

Oh, they had put animosity on hold a little when they had returned to the palace, but the harsh words exchanged before still hummed in her head and she held her palm and remembered the stinging blow she had delivered.

They were both better than that, Maggie knew.

It was not how they should end.

Maggie looked at the time and saw that it was after midnight.

In a few short hours, Kumu would be here to wake her up. Maggie knew that she should try to get some sleep but even as she lay on the bed she knew there was no chance of that.

There was the ache of need and the pull of desire that had her climbing out of bed.

She put on her bikini and marvelled at the smoothness of her skin from her afternoon in the *hammam*. She covered herself with the small wrap towel.

Maggie knew that she should not be considering trying to find Ilyas, yet she decided that if caught, she would simply say that she had decided to go for a swim.

But there was another reason that she should not be venturing here, Maggie knew as she negotiated the ancient labyrinth that ran beneath the palace.

She might not like what she found when she got there!

CHAPTER TEN

THE TUNNELS WERE candlelit, but it was the sound of running water that guided her.

She passed the area where she had been pampered earlier that day and remembered being told to go and rinse off. Maggie followed, as best she could, the same path she had taken then.

Yet it was not memory that drew her now, or the sound of cascading water in the distance. Instead, it was the fragrant, sensual air and the other sounds—music mingled with women's laughter—that told her she was nearing the forbidden part of the *hammam*.

And then the blue tiles gave way to crimson and she entered the forbidden passageway.

Maggie could hear the women's laughter and chatter fading as she walked in the opposite direction of their sounds.

She looked up at the rope that ran the length of the passage and wondered if he had already summoned his choice for the night.

Or choice*s*.

She stopped at one of the tiny fonts and this time when she pressed her fingers in she did not just inhale the fragrance. Instead, she rubbed it on her neck and chest, wondering if that was what *they* did.

Of course not, Maggie thought, made more than aware of her own naivety as she looked at the murals. The oil was for sex.

The women were sensual and bold and, Maggie could see, would arrive for him all oiled and ready.

It was a daunting thought but she refused to oil herself *there* for him and instead pulled the wrap tighter around her body.

She should not venture further. Maggie knew that. It would kill her to find him in the midst of making love to these beautiful, experienced women.

It was not some masochistic need that kept her walking; it was the pure and desperate hope of seeing him one more time.

Knowing him just a little more.

And even if she did not understand all their ways, she was beginning to.

Maggie reached the end of the passageway, but she crushed her body against the wall and stayed hidden by the shadows. Tentatively, she peered out.

There was a deep, sunken pool and steam rose from the water as it hit the cool night air. There was a fountain that ran down one wall. The guides had been right; the pool at its base glowed red.

And then she saw the true reason she was there and her throat squeezed tight.

Beside the mysterious fountain, on a stone bench that had been carved into a wall, lounged Ilyas, outstretched and propped up on one arm.

His top half was naked but on his bottom half he was

dressed in black, silk harem pants that lay low on his hips. Her eyes travelled down the length of him, from his beautiful chiselled face to his bare feet.

She was glad that he was alone and grateful to have this moment. This was how she would remember him.

She jolted at the deep sound of his voice.

'You're late.'

Maggie stepped out of the tunnel, and though the air was cool her face was hot.

'How did you know I'd come?' Maggie asked.

'I didn't,' he said, and then her stomach twisted as he admitted more. 'But I hoped.'

There was so much they could say, but that was not the reason she was there. It was a deep desire for his body that had pulled her from her bed, not the need to talk.

He summoned her with his finger but it seemed a very long walk around the pool on legs that felt like jelly.

She stopped before she reached him, and stood by the pool instead.

'What if someone comes?'

'They wouldn't dare without my summons,' he told her, but that made Maggie feel no better. Occasional echoes of laughter still carried from the harem, and the music, though distant, beat like a pulse through her. 'You're overdressed for the *hammam*,' he told her.

Maggie knew that she was.

But she felt more than just overdressed; she felt ill-equipped to be in such a sensual space, one where even the water ran red.

One night with the Sheikh was all she had known but, oh, how she wanted more! Instead, she stood frozen by her own inexperience.

And though Ilyas wanted her to come closer, her hesitation was fetching.

'If you don't undress,' Ilyas told her, 'I will insist again that you dance.'

And then he smiled and Maggie found that she did too, and the fear lessened.

He watched as she undid the wrap, and when it dropped to the floor he saw she was dressed in the bikini she had worn in the photos.

Ilyas had wanted her on sight and his body's response to her creamy flesh was the same as it had been even before they'd met.

In fact, it was heightened, for he now knew every inch of that body. He had tasted her deep and had climaxed to her moans.

'Come here,' he told her again, though with impatience now, for he was not used to delivering an order twice.

But again she did not comply.

He stood and stepped out of the black harem pants. The sight of him naked still made her nervous, albeit deliciously so. He was erect, hugely so, and that stunning body was primed for action. She felt as if a hand had slipped into her stomach and was squeezing her tight; even her lungs did not seem able to drag in the cold night air at the sight of him so potently ready for her.

They eyed each other from opposite sides of the pool and when Maggie still did not make her way over on his command, Ilyas dived in and she watched as he powerfully stroked through the water towards her.

Ilyas rose and stood, the surface of the water caressing his chest in small, choppy waves. She wondered if he would grab at her ankle or climb from the pool.

He did neither.

She felt cruelly denied now that the water had stolen his glorious body from her view. A surge of confidence had her accept that she was past being shy with him.

Always she had hidden her nakedness.

Her gypsy life had meant a lot of new bathrooms, and it was always in there that Maggie dressed.

Not here in Zayrinia.

And not tonight.

Maggie lifted her hands and slipped them behind her back, undoing the knot, then she pulled off the top of her bikini. She liked the alert gaze of his eyes on her body and the heat of tense impatience that transcended the cool night air.

Then she slipped down the bikini bottom and stepped out of it. Finally she took a step forward to join him in the pool.

'Stay there a moment,' he told her, for he wanted to capture her naked beauty and remember this vision for ever.

Her teeth pressed into her bottom lip as she fought not to touch herself. Her breasts ached and her tender sex throbbed with want.

Ilyas watched for a moment until he could no longer resist her. He held out his hands and without a word she slipped into the water.

The water was delicious—warm, even a little hot. Her foot briefly met the stone floor but he was waiting and his arm pulled her that last distance towards him. She lost her footing so there was no firm ground beneath her, only the solid feel of Ilyas and their wet, naked skin slithering together.

He claimed her mouth and this time did not wait for

her lips to part; he forced in his tongue and pulled her close. His kiss was rough and savage but so was Maggie's. Her anger, the impending loss were drowned out with the frenzied exchange of their mouths.

She coiled her legs tight around his bottom and kissed him back with all the passion the future denied them.

But then he slowed them down, kissing her softly. The gentle stroke of his tongue and the soft caress of his hands swept her body with tender passion that felt very different from their night in the tent in the desert.

He was so strong and she ran her hands over his muscled arms as he first held her waist, then slipped down and cupped her buttocks.

The veil of water kept their secret and Maggie rested her head on his shoulder as her eyes screwed closed. She was hot and swollen from last night and as he squeezed in it was almost as painful as before. She pressed her teeth into his shoulder and tasted salt with her tongue; she bit down a little and then they were one.

Their kisses were slow now as he moved within her.

'You belong here, Maggie,' he told her.

She felt as if she did.

Maggie's head felt too heavy for her neck, and when she stretched it he kissed her there, moving faster and faster, driving into her with his thick length.

His fingers dug into willing flesh as their eyes locked. Both gazed deeply into each other's eyes, reading the flames of desire and the smoke of anger and the white-hot heat of intense want.

She held her hands behind his head and shifted her hips in seductive slow motions. His lips tightened as he fought the urge to thrust hard and end this complex union, for this was more than sex, and he could not tear his eyes from hers.

Her breasts slid on his chest and the steam and the heat they made had her slippery and moving with utter ease. Maggie felt as fluid as the water, unlocked and undone, and so open to sensation that when he took over the rhythm and started pounding into her she simply handed her body over to him.

He thrust with precision, watching her mouth spread and the cords on her neck tighten as he took her faster. Her thighs were shaking as her calves gripped behind his back. She could feel his final surge and then, as Ilyas unleashed that raw, male power, she came with a sob and clenched him tightly as he drove his precious drops deep within her.

Maggie rested her head on his shoulder, fulfilled, but sad that it was over.

'Come on,' he said, but he did not lower her; instead, he carried her and placed her on the pool's edge. She watched as, with practised ease, he climbed out.

'Let's go to the ledge…'

He had told her about that, about how it was his favourite space, and that no one else was permitted there. She was almost scared to be shown more of his world.

Because she was afraid of what this meant; of how it would feel when she had to leave.

But of course she said yes.

CHAPTER ELEVEN

THEY WALKED HAND in hand.

He pulled down some ornate carpets, which they lay on, then he covered them both in a rug. They lay on the ledge and looked up at the magnificent sky.

It had never, Ilyas thought, looked better than it did tonight. It was as if every star had been polished to sparkle just for her.

'I'm glad you got to see it like this,' he said.

'So am I.'

She had been almost reluctant to join him. For the sake of her heart it would have been safer to go back to bed, but instead she stared up at the exquisite sky and was so glad she had been brave.

Yes, brave, Maggie thought, because there were so many sides to Ilyas, and she was caught between wanting to know him better and knowing they must soon part.

'How often do you come here?' Maggie asked.

'Usually when there is no moon, or a new moon like this—it is easier that way to see stars.'

That hadn't been what she had meant.

Maggie had wanted to know how often he visited the *hammam*, but she was glad he had misunderstood, for on reflection she didn't want to know the answer.

Ilyas had not misunderstood.

He didn't want to tell her the truth, that most of his nights were spent here, but neither did he want to lie to her.

Her hair was wet and it trailed across his head as Maggie lifted herself up a bit and looked back at where they had been.

'Rubies?' she asked. She had just now worked out the real secret of the red river.

He nodded.

'So there was no prince who lost his head…?'

'There was,' Ilyas said, and knew that if he wasn't careful, there could well be another one. He pulled her back to his arms. 'His lover wanted a necklace made of rubies. Of course he arranged that, but she insisted that the stones come from the cave pool—more than that, she insisted he be the one to mine them. It is deep,' he told Maggie.

She loved lying in his arms and hearing the tales told in his rich, deep voice.

'He was warned of the risk and the danger, yet by then he cared nothing for what they said. His sole aim was to please her, and so he dived over and over, until he was exhausted and weak and, of course, he died.'

'She sounds very demanding,' Maggie said, making him smile.

'Consequently, if the crown prince wishes to choose his own bride, he must make the same dive, or accept the choice of the palace elders and the king. Only a fool would risk his life for love.'

'I guess.' Maggie sighed. 'Did Hazin dive for Petra?'

'He is not crown prince.'

'But did he?'

'I don't wish to discuss it.'

Maggie breathed out. So many subjects were closed. 'Do you still think something went on between him and me?' she asked.

'I know that nothing went on,' Ilyas said. 'I believed you, or we would not have—' He halted, because he had been about to say *made love*. Instead, he told her what had happened that day. 'Mahmoud is spinning in fear. I tried to speak with Hazin but he has gone to ground. Another threat was made at lunchtime...'

'From Suzanne?'

'Apparently. She says that the tapes are set to be aired at midday, and she went into some rather salacious details.' He smiled down as Maggie looked up and frowned at his calm reaction. 'I was concerned, as I believe Hazin is, that they might have recorded your conversation. If that were the case, then reluctantly I might have had to consider their demands. However, you and I know that nothing untoward happened and they clearly don't have a recording of voices, or they would be using that to bribe us now. The yacht has been checked and it would seem a camera might have been placed in a vent over the bed. There would have been no sound. It must be a rather boring few hours of footage...'

They both laughed and the sound of them joyful together was more beautiful than any sound Maggie had ever heard. 'I was sitting on a desk, chatting. Hazin was lounging on the bed...'

It was funny, really, to think of Suzanne and whoever else tearing their hair out at the complete lack of action.

And then their laughter faded and she knew what was coming, for the night was fast leaving them.

'Stay,' Ilyas said.

Maggie swallowed. 'For how long?'

He didn't answer and so Maggie drew her own conclusion. 'Until you get tired of me.'

'I didn't say that,' Ilyas responded, but she pulled from his embrace and sat up.

'But you shall.'

It had happened on too many occasions in her life for her not to believe it now, but Ilyas denied it would be like that.

'You would be beautifully looked after,' he told her.

She would be his on-call lover, Maggie knew. She looked up at the velvet rope that hung above them.

'I don't answer to bells,' Maggie said.

'I would send Kumu for you, then.'

His answer was so wrong but so telling. Clearly, she would not be in his bed; she would just be summoned when he so desired. It would not be a partnership, a relationship. It would just be sex, and it would all be on *his* terms.

'What if you *don't* grow tired of me?' Maggie asked.

'Maggie…' Ilyas shook his head, refusing to get into that, but Maggie was insistent.

'No, answer me. What if, say, a year from now, we're still sitting under the stars at night and still feeling as we do now?'

He didn't answer, and she was glad of that. Unlike the foster family that had finally broken her, he did not say the right thing in the moment and make promises he had no intention of keeping.

'Can we ever be more than this?' Maggie asked. 'More than just lovers?'

In truth, he had never considered there ever being more to them than this. He was a lone wolf. Yes, he would marry, but that would be to produce an heir. Certainly the loving relationship she alluded to was not part of his plan, and so he answered her honestly.

'No.'

He didn't sweeten it, he did not lie, and Maggie admired him for that. She had been lied to so many times in her life that promises had little meaning.

She looked up at the sky that was changing too fast. Stars were disappearing, like the lights being turned off one by one as a building was vacated. She knew it was time to leave.

'I'd better get back. Kumu will be coming for me soon.'

'Not yet,' Ilyas said, for he wanted to have her again. But she avoided his kiss and climbed from his arms. 'Maggie!' he called, but she headed back to the pool and started collecting her things.

'Stay,' he said again. 'Even just for a few days. I will arrange another flight.'

'I want *that* flight,' Maggie said. 'My mother paid for it.'

'You're being sentimental.'

'Yes,' Maggie said, and she stood and pulled on the tiny bikini she had so readily discarded. 'And I intend to remain so.' She looked at the man who didn't get the little things that made her heart beat in time. 'I'm going home today, because you think you can send a maid to knock on my door because you want sex. This conversation is pointless.'

'What do you want?' he asked. 'I've told you there can be no marriage, my father would never—'

'You really think I want to marry you?' Maggie checked. 'Just to give you an heir? No, Ilyas, it's a partnership I want and conversation. A relationship,' she said, 'but you don't do that.'

'We're talking now,' Ilyas returned.

'I mean real conversation. You're more than willing to listen to stories I tell you, but you tell me so little about yourself.'

'That's not true,' Ilyas refuted, for he had shared with her things he never discussed with anyone.

'Let's talk about your brother, then,' Maggie said as she pulled on her little top and flicked out her hair. 'Come on.'

'Leave it.'

'Or,' Maggie suggested, 'we could talk about Petra...'

'Maggie!'

'Okay, too personal. What about what you're going to be doing today?'

'I have meetings in the morning.'

'About what?'

'Things that do not concern you,' Ilyas said. He was not used to sharing and did not know how to do it.

'So what am I to do if I stay?'

'I've told you, you would be beautifully looked after.'

'You mean I'd while my days away in the *hammam* getting ready for sex on demand with you!'

'And what is wrong with that?'

For a beat, for a second, Maggie waited for his smile to tell her that he was joking, but then she realised the absolute arrogance of the man—Ilyas meant every word.

Worse, though, despite the fury at him that was coursing through Maggie, there was something else too. She was angry at herself for considering it.

'Oh, I should have saved that slap for now!' Maggie

snarled, but her real anger was not aimed at him. Yes, the thought of being his lover and living this luxurious life still danced in her mind, still tempted her with its dazzling promise, and she was precariously close to saying yes.

She went to walk away but he followed her and caught her wrist.

'We haven't finished,' he told her.

'Yes, we have!' Maggie cried. Though she loathed his words, she loathed herself more.

Lust gripped her tighter than the hand on her wrist, but it was Ilyas who started to kiss her.

It was a raw kiss, a persuasive kiss, and so intense that it pushed her so her back was to the stone wall.

There was not an inch of her that was not willing, for her tongue was tussling with his. Maggie wanted this kiss, and she wanted the tug of his hands as he shredded the bikini she had just replaced.

But even as her body craved him—and maybe it would for ever—she had learnt long ago to guard her heart, and she knew this could only serve to hurt her further.

'I have to go.'

'Not yet…'

She was turned on and so too was he; she could feel him pressed hard into her. It would be the easiest thing to sink into his kiss, to be taken again.

But that had got her nowhere other than to make leaving more difficult.

It was the hardest but bravest thing she had ever done, but Maggie pushed him away.

They faced each other, their breathing harsh. Oh, how much easier, so much easier, it would be to give in, for their bodies were on fire with want. She could see his erection and its glistening silver tip. He saw her look and his hand came up to the back of her head. Maggie felt so drunk and dizzy with lust that she wanted to sink to her knees.

'Do you want to come?' Maggie checked, and she licked her lips seductively.

'Of course I do.'

'Fine then.'

But instead of lowering her head, Maggie lifted her arm and pulled on the rope. She heard the sounds of bells and then gave Ilyas her blackest smile as she ran her hand down his impressive length. 'Someone will be along to take care of that in a minute.'

As Maggie walked off she heard footsteps running along the passage and the sound of approaching bells as someone rushed to take care of the master.

She turned and saw his furious expression. Maggie laughed out loud.

Better that than to cry.

CHAPTER TWELVE

'WHERE WERE YOU?'

Kumu was wide-eyed with worry when Maggie returned to the suite.

'I just went for a swim,' Maggie said, and forced herself to smile.

'Well, I have laid out some clothes for you to choose from,' Kumu told her. 'I shall leave you to get dressed and have your luggage taken to the car and then I shall come and do your hair.'

'I can manage.'

'Maggie,' she said, 'when you are a guest of Crown Prince Ilyas you don't have to *manage*.'

Kumu left her then and Maggie stood alone in the suite, looking out at a beautiful Zayrinian dawn.

She truly was tired of managing.

Maggie was bone tired with trying to find her place in this world that had denied her over and over the one thing she wanted more than anything—a family.

Rarely did she admit it, even to herself, but her breath shuddered as she accepted the truth. Maggie knew she was perilously close to breaking down.

She was scared to, though, for if the tears started they might never stop.

She wanted to stay, she wanted to be looked after, she wanted never to have to *manage* again.

Oh, no, you don't, Maggie told herself.

Oh, yes she did.

But more than that, so much more than that, she wanted to *matter*.

Maggie wanted his love.

If she stayed, it would be with the hope that he would come to love her, and that would be a foolish reason to remain. Maggie knew she could not stay, wishing things would change, all the while waiting for him to tire of the challenge of her.

She could not risk the agony of rejection.

And it would be worse than it had been with Diane, because Maggie hadn't loved her. But she did love Ilyas.

And he would never return it.

No, he would marry eventually and disband the harem. Ilyas had told her that himself.

It was better to leave now on her own terms than live entirely under his.

She could not stand to be *his* living doll.

Or rather his live-in doll.

With her mind made up, Maggie looked at the robes set out for her. The clothes, the hair, the pampering were not for her enjoyment but so that she could be presentable for him, Maggie now knew.

She would have refused to wear a robe except that her backpack had been taken to the car.

Maggie selected the first one she touched. It was a mink velvet, which would likely clash with her red hair. Well, bad luck, Ilyas!

Yet, when she slipped it on, it worked.

She put jewelled slippers on her feet and then Kumu

came to the door with make-up and brushes and a bag of tricks to make her *presentable* for the future king.

'I don't want my hair done,' Maggie said.

'But your curls need to be tamed,' Kumu insisted.

'I like them,' Maggie said, and she saw Kumu's rapid blink.

'I shall do your make-up, then.'

'No, thank you,' Maggie said. 'The crown prince will just have to take me as I am this morning and, believe me, having my hair and make-up done is the furthest thing from my mind.'

Instead of insisting, Kumu's face broke into a wide smile. 'Good for you.'

'Thank you for everything,' Maggie said. She had taken a gift from her bag that she had actually bought for Flo. It was a silver bracelet that she had watched being made, but she had other presents for Flo and knew that her friend would understand.

Kumu was delighted and slipped the bangle on and then, to Maggie's surprise, gave her a hug. 'I am going to miss you.'

'But I've only been here for a day,' Maggie said.

'I know, but the palace was so happy to have you here.'

She spoke of the building as if it were a person. Maggie got that, for it did feel a little like she was being torn from her moorings as she headed down a huge stairwell. This place felt more like home than any she had known since the morning when she'd been a child and the lights had snapped on in her room and she had been hauled from her bed.

But now it was time for her to leave.

There was no sign of Ilyas and she was led through

corridors she had not had time to explore to a large foyer that looked rather like the entrance to a luxurious hotel.

And, no, Ilyas was not waiting for her.

Ilyas had been sulking.

He had angrily sent away the woman that Maggie had summoned when she'd stormed out of the *hammam*. He was furious at what she had done, furious that she had reduced their connection to sex. Even though that was all it had been between them. Right? That was what he had told himself; that was what he had told her.

He did not usually head out to say farewell to lovers and certainly he was cross. But she had changed him perhaps more than she knew, for he put his own anger on hold.

In fact, it had gone the second he'd walked into the foyer and seen her standing there, talking to Kumu.

No one spoke here, not really.

No one stood chatting for no reason, yet Kumu was telling Maggie about her daughter, and how well she was doing at school.

Idle gossip perhaps, but friendly conversation was something badly lacking within these walls.

Kumu suddenly stopped speaking and Maggie saw the reason why when she turned.

There he stood, dressed in a black robe and *kafeyah*; unlike Maggie, he was all polished and groomed.

'Could you excuse us?' Ilyas said to Kumu, instead of dismissing her with his usual wave.

And then he and Maggie stood facing each other.

'How was your morning?' Maggie asked.

'Confusing for some,' Ilyas said, referring to the woman she had summoned whom he had immediately shooed away, 'and frustrating for others,' he added, meaning himself.

'Good.' Maggie smiled, glad for the little bit of chaos she had caused.

Ilyas could not read her. He looked at the tumble of red curls and her unmade-up face and thought that she had never been more beautiful to him than she was now.

He was certain she did not want to leave and yet she stood there with a smile.

And he was equally certain he did not want her to leave, though he knew she was right to—he did not want her whiling away her days in the *hammam*.

His father would never consider her a suitable bride, and neither would the palace elders.

Love was not part of the plan for a future king.

Ilyas had never once doubted his future.

That he would be king had been decided before conception. He had been born for just that after all.

And every day of his life he had planned for it.

Yet today it felt like nothing more than painful duty because he wanted to cancel the car and summon the jet and whisk them both away.

Ilyas rarely took a day off, but a holiday away from the palace with Maggie, watching her pale skin turn bronze, teasing her into submission...

He looked at Maggie, all set to leave, and couldn't help himself asking again for more time.

'What if we went away for a few days?'

'Where?'

'Anywhere.'

He offered her heaven, but she had already checked the small print of his offer.

'No, thank you.'

One day, hopefully not too far from now, she would try to fathom just how it felt to be so drawn to someone while at the same time knowing she had to leave.

Maggie had learnt not to get upset at goodbyes.

They had all been a rehearsal for this morning, for it was by far the hardest goodbye of her life.

He walked her out through a large doorway to an area where the car waited to take her to the airport.

There were other cars too, some leaving and some arriving, like a very exclusive taxi rank, as the palace and its people went about a busy working day.

She would miss this for ever.

He saw her right to the waiting car.

'Thank you for kidnapping me,' Maggie said, making him smile.

'And thank you for *not* being Suzanne.'

That made her laugh just a little.

He had made her laugh and he craved more of that sound. No, humour was not his forte, yet he was discovering it just to see more of her smile.

'Ilyas…'

He turned briefly at the sound of his name and so too did Maggie.

It was her first sight of the king.

Maggie knew that it was him, just as she had known, when first she'd seen Ilyas, that he was a leader. King Ahmed was walking with some of the palace elders; perhaps that was how he did his business, Maggie mused.

He was as dismissive of Maggie as his wife, the queen, had been, for he paid no attention to her, just spoke in Arabic to his son and then went to walk inside.

'Ilyas!' he called out to his son again, clearly expecting him to follow him in, but Ilyas refused to be rushed and continued to speak with Maggie.

'Have you got everything?' Ilyas checked.

She went into her purse and pulled out her itinerary and passport. 'All here.'

Maggie looked at the itinerary, with all her flights ticked off bar one. How well she remembered the day she had printed it off, knowing full well that discovery awaited, while never really expecting to fall in love.

But she had. Deeply.

'Have a safe flight,' Ilyas said.

There was no promise to see each other again.

He didn't even lie and say they might keep in touch.

It really was goodbye and both knew that it really had to be.

'Oh, here,' Ilyas said, and reached into his deep pockets, then handed her her phone. 'There isn't much charge. They only just got it running.'

'I'm sure you've been through it.'

'No.'

She looked up then. 'Why not?'

'Because I know you would hate it if I did.'

'Thank you,' she said, and then smiled. 'I shall be going through it, though. I want to know what Suzanne said...' She turned it on and tried to make light of the situation. In fact, Maggie did all she could to pretend this was just another goodbye amongst the many.

'There's nothing,' Maggie said as she scrolled through her phone.

'She would have deleted as she went along.'

But then all thoughts of Suzanne were gone as her phone started to go crazy as message after message pinged in.

'It's Paul,' she said, 'he's worried that I haven't responded to his emails.' She read on. 'He's offered me a promotion if I come back!'

And then she laughed but choked in the midst of it as she read on. 'Flo's been trying to get hold of me. She's threatening to contact Interpol if I don't get in touch soon.'

It was so wonderful to know that she had friends who cared deeply.

Who had noticed she was gone.

'It would seem I was missed after all.'

'Of course you were.'

He had never doubted that she would be, Maggie thought, not for a second. That night when she had felt so lonely, he had told her how important she surely was to the people in her life.

And he showed her that now.

To hell with protocol, and even with his father, for he took her in his arms.

'You shall be missed by me.'

Then don't let me go, she wanted to beg. *Offer me more than time as your whore*, she wanted to plead, but she was saved from begging by his mouth.

His kiss was pure Ilyas.

There was no discreet brush of the lips. Instead, he devoured.

His eyes were closed as he swept her to the most bittersweet bliss—for he kissed her so hard and so fiercely, with all the passion that her leaving denied them.

And it was not a kiss to which she could fail to respond.

He pulled her tight against him, and her hands went up around his neck as he tasted her again with his tongue.

It was a deep and sensual kiss, slow and measured, and he was the only one who could melt her like this.

Right now, Maggie thought, she would have to fight to muster a protest if he tipped her over his shoulder and carried her to his bed.

Yet halt they must, and they rested their foreheads together for a moment until it was time to part.

Stunned by his overt affection, she was guided to the open car door.

She must not look back, Maggie thought as the car door closed. Almost immediately, the vehicle started to move away.

But she did. She couldn't help herself.

And there he was, standing tall and still and watching her leave.

He did not wave.

It was a unique agony. One she had never experienced before.

It felt like love, but if it was, then why the hell was she leaving? And why was he letting her go?

Because love wasn't on his agenda.

It was a horrible pill to swallow.

The bitterest of them all.

Somehow, sometime soon, she would be able to relegate this weekend to a holiday romance, Maggie told herself.

She just couldn't do that now.

But the holiday really was over.

As she was let out at Zayrinia Airport, Maggie knew she had to adjust to a world that wasn't in tune with her broken heart, and so she smiled as she handed over her passport at the check-in desk and lifted her backpack onto the belt to be weighed.

'It's your lucky day,' she was told.

It didn't feel like it.

It didn't even feel like it when she was handed a first-class ticket home, and instead of scrabbling for coins for coffee, sat in the first-class lounge, being served delicacies and champagne.

It was lovely, and she knew it was Ilyas who had arranged it.

Her mother's loving gift that he had somehow made better.

But it wasn't the champagne, or the golden pyjamas and flat bed that cocooned her heart as the plane carried her home.

There was another person in her life now.

Another finger on her hand—a person that Maggie could truly say she loved.

CHAPTER THIRTEEN

THE PALACE FELT like a mausoleum after she had gone. Ilyas went to his office and stood looking out of the vast windows that offered panoramic views.

He looked not to the desert, or to the ocean, or to the city spread out beneath him.

Instead, he looked to the sky and wondered if every plane that flashed silver above might be the one that carried her.

'Your Highness.' Mahmoud came in just before twelve. 'It is almost midday.'

'So?'

'The deadline.'

'Ah, yes.'

But it was not the blackmailer's deadline that Mahmoud was here to warn him of.

Ilyas had many people working behind the scenes, and at five minutes after twelve he was duly told that the group who had been threatening the palace had been arrested.

That night, the contents of the tapes were revealed. Mahmoud and the detectives were mightily relieved that they, in fact, contained nothing, but as Ilyas reviewed them, his wretched emotions had nothing to do with the clear proof nothing had happened.

He saw, but could not hear, the conversation.

How she laughed but never cried and how, away from the palace, just how much more relaxed Hazin appeared.

And then, because he had to, Ilyas set to work.

In the coming months Ilyas threw himself into his plans and his problems and worked harder than he ever had.

He was away more often than not, though he avoided Europe and particularly London.

There was much to be done!

When home, he still visited the *hammam*, but the velvet cord remained unused, for the focus of his desire remained Maggie, and even a sky full of stars seemed empty when gazed upon without her.

There was plenty to keep him busy, though.

Hazin and his latest escapades, for one.

His brother was like black confetti, gracing the covers of magazines with tell-all tales of the Bachelor Prince who would not be tamed.

And, despite Ilyas's efforts to speak with him, his brother refused to meet. As well as that, Hazin had point-blank refused the king's final demand to return home.

Ilyas left the *hammam* just close to sunrise.

He walked up the steps until the bedrock changed to marble and then he went and prayed.

After that, he called for his dresser and then, alone, he checked his reflection.

He looked as he always looked.

And then he looked out at the desert and it too looked the same.

Ilyas picked up a stone from the dresser and placed it into his deep pocket, and as he left the room he gave it a rare backward glance.

Ilyas walked down a long hallway on his way to a meeting with his father and paused to look at the huge portrait of Hazin and Petra on their wedding day.

They both looked so young. They had been, then.

Eighteen.

He recalled the time she had died and the grief that had swept through the nation.

His father's answer?

That Ilyas marry and produce an heir, as if that would appease the people.

He had told his father to allow the people to grieve in their own time. Yet, while wise to the needs of his people, he hadn't been able to offer the same to Hazin.

They were not close, for they had never been allowed to be close.

They had never really discussed it and the palace had moved on—Petra's death had become an item on a meeting agenda.

In fact, she was on it today, for the ten-year anniversary was approaching.

Hazin was expected to return for it and to open a new wing at the hospital.

Named after a princess they had been unable to save.

Ilyas saw the guards outside his father's office and knew that the swords they held were not for decoration. As he awaited the opening of the doors, he drew in a long breath and held it a moment.

Ilyas was ready.

He walked into the meeting and saw Mahmoud present, as well as several palace elders. It was clear that his father had plans for a long meeting.

Well, Ilyas would see about that.

A lifetime of plans in the making were coming to fruition now.

Ilyas took a seat at the large table, facing his father.

First they spoke of international issues and there were plenty of them.

Ilyas held onto his temper as he found out that a fledgling truce with a neighbouring land he had worked hard to broker was now under threat thanks to his father's poor handling of a trivial incident.

'They need to be shown,' King Ahmed said.

Screw you, Ilyas thought, but remained silent for now.

They moved on to more local matters and the protests in town from the tour operators who wanted more desert access.

'Their livelihoods are threatened,' the king said. 'For the sake of a couple of miles of sand we could help them prosper.'

'No.' Ilyas spoke. 'They have asked for more than a couple of miles.'

'Only to take the elite out,' his father said. 'The tourist industry is an important one. The Bedouins have to accept that.'

It was a complex problem, and not for the first time he missed Maggie, for so much more than just her glorious body. It was *her*, it was Maggie that he missed. Her conversation and discussing issues, a valued person's slant on things that he had found he needed when he had never thought he would.

And he thought of her now as he spoke.

'Why don't we discuss it with them?' Ilyas suggested.

'I have met with some of their senior elders—' Mahmoud started, but Ilyas overrode him.

'Why is there not a Bedouin representative at this table?' Ilyas asked. 'This motion shall be debated in full at a later date and with a senior representative from them at this table. Next item.'

There was silence.

'Next,' Ilyas said again. He could feel his father's rage coming across the table and there was slight panic in Mahmoud's voice as he attempted to move things along swiftly and divert King Ahmed's response.

'The new oncology wing is nearing completion,' Mahmoud said. 'I am working on Hazin's speech—'

'Shouldn't it be Princess Petra's family who delivers it?' Ilyas interrupted.

'Hazin is her family,' King Ahmed said, and his voice was pure ice, for he was just getting over his shock at his son's high-handed attempt to take control of the meeting. At first he had been too stunned to respond to it, but now he asserted his dominance. 'If he wants to remain a prince, he shall deliver the speech.'

'But your younger son is clearly struggling,' Ilyas said.

The older one was not.

Ilyas had thought this day might be years off yet, but his time with Maggie had brought that day forward.

And that day was now!

'Right now, I don't have a younger son.' King Ahmed spat out his words. 'Hazin disgusts me. He is barely holding onto his title. If he wants to be a member of the royal family, he needs to act accordingly.'

'Our title is wrong,' Ilyas corrected. 'We are royal but not a family.'

'Next,' King Ahmed said, since it was he who wanted

this meeting to be over and done with now. 'The meeting is adjourned.'

'No, it's not,' Ilyas said, and as everyone went to stand and get out, Ilyas gestured for them all to be re-seated. 'Mahmoud,' he said. 'Please take careful notes.'

A hush fell around the room and Ilyas looked directly at his father. 'I am leaving this afternoon for London,' he said. 'There I shall speak with my brother and try to gauge the best way to deal with the anniversary of Princess Petra's death. Who knows, I might even ask for his input.' And then he recalled his conversations with Maggie and added, 'That's sarcasm, by the way.'

It was a pure threat to King Ahmed's leadership, it was an absolute refusal to back down, and the king knew it. He flung back his chair and stood.

'Then let me remind you who is king.'

Ilyas ignored his father's outburst and remained seated. In fact, he calmly examined his nails as if bored by his father's drama.

And then he put down his hand and Ilyas made his move.

'There is to be a transition of power.'

There was an audible gasp from those present, though Ilyas spoke on as if he were discussing the traffic issue in front of the palace. 'It will be a gentle transition, but I shall take on more responsibility, and all future decisions are to be approved by me.'

'Get out!' his father shouted. 'Now, before I call the guards.'

'If you insist,' Ilyas said, and he stood, 'but we both know that one day I shall be king and when I am—'

King Ahmed did not let him speak. 'I shall have you arrested. You can't be king locked in a tower.'

'Then who will be?' Ilyas asked. 'You have stripped the tree of its fruit. Hazin won't do it and I have no heir, so that leaves your brother and his fat, idle offspring.' Ilyas knew that his father hated his brother; there was no love for anyone in his parents' black hearts. 'So stand there withered and bare, you foolish old man, and watch me take it to the people. This is no idle threat,' he warned his father. 'I have taken one piece of your advice and I have always looked forward. My brother, God willing, will serve by my side, and certainly this country shall move forward and heal from the many mistakes you have made.'

'Get out!' his father screeched, but, Ilyas noted, King Ahmed did not call for guards, for he knew, as Ilyas had pointed out, there was no option other than him moving forward.

'Gladly,' Ilyas agreed. 'As I said, I am going to London to speak with my brother.'

'Then tell Hazin from me that from this day forward if he chooses to live a reckless life then it shall be without his deep, royal pocket. There shall be no security, no royal jet, no chauffeur—no one to catch him as he falls from grace.'

'I shall be there for him,' Ilyas said. 'And,' he added, 'I hope to return with my future bride. You won't approve of her, but I don't need your approval.' He gave his father a black smile. 'Know that from this day forward it is you who needs my approval.'

It was done.

There was no going back and Ilyas nodded to the guards as he made his way out.

'Your Highness…' Mahmoud had to run to catch up

with him. 'You cannot threaten a coup and then leave the country.'

'No coup.' Ilyas shook his head. 'There is no need for that yet. As I said to my father, it will be a gentle transition. Perhaps you and the elders might delicately suggest to him the same. Failing that, there *shall* be a coup. I shan't ask if I have you onside. I do not ask you to disrespect our king—yet.'

He gave the old man his first ever smile from a leader and walked away.

Ilyas knew that he had Mahmoud onside.

For, yes, he had planned this day for many years.

Decades in fact.

He was disciplined and had bided his time until he could properly see it through.

He had just never factored into his grand plans having a wife by his side.

And certainly not one called Maggie.

CHAPTER FOURTEEN

MAGGIE HAD SPENT the last few months disproving her theory that you could never get sick of chocolate.

Her long-held belief was wrong.

The taste was too sweet and the very scent of it had started to make her stomach curl.

Flo had been the one who had told her she was pregnant.

Maggie would have happily remained in la-la land for a few more weeks, and had put her vomiting down to a bug she had brought home from her trip.

Except she had been borrowing Flo's sofa at the time.

And, given that Flo was a practising midwife, her friend's confident diagnosis had been rather hard to ignore.

Maggie had tried to!

She had found a flat that offered a little more privacy than Maggie was used to. While she would be sharing the bathroom and kitchen with four others, there was a little room with a sofa and bed and there were locks on that door.

After a year of travelling and a lifetime of shared lounge rooms, there was finally a glimmer of privacy and peace.

Flo had helped her move in.

It was tiny and seriously needed a fresh coat of paint, but they had prettied it up with pictures on the walls and thrown a few rugs over the couch.

Next to Maggie's bed there was a built-in shelf, and she decided that this would be the spot where she placed her favourite things, as she always did when she started again in a new home.

There was a gorgeous photo of herself and her mum taken the Christmas before she had died, which she carefully placed in the centre of the shelf.

Beside that she put an empty bottle of expensive perfume—it had been a present from Paul and Kelly when she had been their bridesmaid and was far too pretty to throw out.

And there was another lovely photo of herself and Flo on Maggie's twenty-first birthday when Flo had organised a surprise party at the café.

Yes, these were her favourite things but there was a new addition to the shelf—a little glass bottle that Maggie had carefully chosen and had bought just yesterday.

It was filled with the sand she had saved from her time in the desert.

That night, with everything unpacked and put away, Flo had produced a bottle of sparkling wine to toast Maggie in her new home.

'No, thanks,' Maggie had said, and had shaken her head.

'I thought you might say that!'

'Please leave it.'

'Maggie, what is that going to achieve? Even if it's just to put my mind at ease, please take a test.'

Flo had produced from her purse a pregnancy testing kit and, on the first night in her new home, Maggie had had it confirmed that she was pregnant.

Of course, she had already suspected. Deep down, she had known it was true, but she'd had no idea what to do, so she had ignored it as best she could.

'How?' Maggie had asked, and there had been rare tears in her eyes as she'd looked around her tiny living space. Flo had understood that she wasn't asking how it had happened, more how she was going to support a baby on her own.

'You'll find a way,' Flo said with conviction. 'You always do.'

She would *manage*, Maggie thought, and closed her eyes, remembering Kumu's words that day, when she'd told her that when in Ilyas's world she didn't have to.

She would barely manage, Maggie knew.

Yes, she might have had a promotion, but a café manager's wage in London wasn't going to change her world and she had no idea how long she'd be able to work into pregnancy.

And after?

She wasn't exactly tripping over relatives who wanted to mind the baby while she went back to work.

It was daunting.

'Could you think about telling the baby's father?' Flo had gently broached the subject, because at that point Maggie had said nothing about Ilyas.

'I can't tell him.'

'He has responsibilities,' Flo had said.

'Absolutely he does,' Maggie had agreed. 'He's going to be king.'

Flo had been shocked.

In fact, she had opened the wine!

'What do you think he'd do if he knew?' Flo had asked over and over again, but the answer was always the same.

'I have no idea,' Maggie had said, over and over. And then she'd made up her mind. 'I don't want him to know.'

Maggie had been too scared of the ramifications if he did.

Now, nearly six months into her pregnancy, Maggie woke before her alarm and looked at the little glass bottle that she had since moved from the shelf to her bedside table.

Every morning when she awoke, he was the person that came first to mind and he continued to dance through her thoughts as she went about her day.

She had managed.

Better than that, with more than a little help from her wonderful friends, Maggie had a future in place.

She had started a course in bookkeeping with the hope of being able to work from home for a while once the baby arrived. Kerry and Paul's son was about to move from his cot to a bed and so that was taken care of. As well as that, she was working every hour possible to save up what she could.

Maggie had found a flat that was a little more baby friendly and in two weeks' time she would be moving.

Again.

Yes, she had plans in place, and the future looked far more secure than it had in those first weeks after she had found out.

Now that she could finally breathe a little easier, her absolute certainty that Ilyas must never know faded.

Her first scan had looked like a blob of grey on grey and Maggie had simply headed straight into work afterwards, still unable to reconcile herself to the fact that she was going to have a baby.

But her second scan, yesterday, had changed all of that.

There was a nose and eyes and fingers and toes and a complete little person on the screen.

'I don't want to know the sex,' Maggie had said, but her tiny baby had taken that decision out of her hands and had waved for the camera.

Maggie was having a boy.

He was a he and already she loved him.

It had been a long night, one of immense soul-searching, and one during which Maggie had done her level best to push her own feelings aside and focus on Ilyas and their son.

She had no family.

None.

And if she didn't at least try to tell Ilyas, she would be all her son had.

Maggie had always wanted to know about her father.

At night, in various care homes, she would fall asleep dreaming of aunts and uncles and cousins that were surely out there somewhere...

Ilyas was so remote, so unreadable that she could not gauge how he would take it.

That morning, she had lain there, feeling her baby fluttering in her tummy and, needing advice, Maggie had texted Flo.

Can you stop by the café on your way to work? I have something to ask you.

* * *

Maggie smiled as her friend came into the café. Flo's blonde hair was tied up and Maggie knew she was on her way to a late shift at the hospital. She didn't need to take her friend's order since it was carved in stone—hot chocolate and a *pain au chocolat*.

'Take your lunch when you're ready,' Paul called.

'Thanks,' Maggie replied, and decided to just take the next customer's order since she had been patiently waiting.

'Can I have a mint hot chocolate, please?' the lady said. 'To go.'

'Sure.' Maggie nodded.

'What's the cake of the day?'

'Dark chocolate and ginger,' Maggie said. 'And I can vouch that it is amazing!'

Yes, her love of chocolate had returned!

She took the lady's order and handed over the change, and it was only then, when the lady held out her hand, that Maggie noticed the white stick that she held in the other and that she was, in fact, blind.

'Enjoy,' Maggie said, placing the money in her palm and then, once she had put it away, handing her the cake and the cup.

Paul had already made up her and Flo's lunches and they soon sat down to their delights as the lady made her way out.

'I didn't realise she was blind when I served her,' Maggie admitted as she watched her skilfully negotiate the glass door.

Flo looked up from adding sugar to her already sweet hot chocolate and watched the lady leave.

How Flo got away with it, Maggie would never know.

She was tiny, even though she ate like a horse and had never set foot in a gym. As well as that she was blonde and gorgeous.

And an utter dating disaster!

Flo attracted bastards more than anyone Maggie had ever met.

Her china-blue eyes seemed to draw them in like moths to a flame.

'She wasn't born blind,' Flo declared.

'Sorry?' Maggie checked.

'If someone is born blind they don't know to know to turn their head towards voices or lift their face to the sun,' Flo explained, 'because they've never seen light or colour. Whereas, if someone loses their sight later on, they've already got the responses.'

'Oh!' Maggie said, as she poured some cream onto her cake. 'You know the most amazing things!'

'Oh, I do. I see that you've got your appetite back!'

'I have,' Maggie agreed, and she took a breath, wondering what Flo's reaction would be when she told her why she'd asked her to drop by.

But Flo thought she had already worked things out.

'I've been thinking,' Flo oh, so, casually said. 'How would you like me to deliver your baby?'

Maggie blinked. She had been half expecting Flo to offer to be her support person, but Maggie was even struggling with the thought of that.

'It would be wonderful,' Flo enthused.

'Absolutely not.' Maggie shook her head, appalled at the very thought. 'No way!'

'But you can't be on your own.'

'I'd prefer to be,' Maggie said.

Yet her heart did a thump as she felt the baby move

again. A deft kick followed by a ripple as if little hummingbirds were fluttering in her stomach.

She didn't want to be on her own.

But it wasn't Flo that she wanted there.

It was Ilyas.

'I thought that was why you asked me here.' Flo slumped.

'I asked you here because I'm thinking that I need to tell Ilyas,' Maggie said. 'I keep being all self-righteous and telling myself it's for the sake of the baby, or that he deserves to know, but the truth is I want him to know and I want the chance to speak to him again.' She took a breath. 'Even if he cares nothing for me.'

If he cared one iota, surely he'd have made some effort to contact her.

Surely?

Yet he hadn't.

And no matter how she examined it, there truly was no excuse, not even that he had no idea where she lived.

He was beyond powerful.

Ilyas could have found her if he'd so chosen.

'Well, it can't come as a complete surprise to him,' Flo said, being practical. 'You used no protection.'

'We were in the *hammam*,' Maggie pointed out.

Yes, Flo had leached out as many details as she possibly could!

'Standing up!' Flo rolled her eyes. 'Please don't tell me you thought that that would stop you getting pregnant?'

'I meant that there weren't exactly condoms handy!' Only that surely wasn't true. She thought of Ilyas in the tent, reaching over to one of many little wooden boxes, and she was certain there would be a supply easily accessible all around the *hammam*. That was, after all, its purpose. She thought about that velvet rope again, and then blushed at Flo's knowing look.

Somehow protection hadn't mattered at the time.

Neither had given it a second's thought.

'How do you think he'll take it?' Flo asked.

'I don't know,' Maggie admitted, and then she thought back. 'He's not exactly open. He thinks being cynical is an asset.'

'You're like that too.'

'At times I can be,' Maggie agreed, 'though I cover it well. I'm still a walk in the park compared to him.' Maggie sighed. 'But sometimes…' She thought about his smile and those rare bursts of laughter. How, when lying chatting with him on cushions or beneath the stars, how open he had been at times and how close to him she had felt.

And then she looked at the glass door and thought about the woman who had just walked through it.

No one would really know she was blind because she had once known the sun.

Just as Maggie had been born knowing love.

Oh, they were long-ago memories, and there were so many forgotten moments, but they came to her at times. Often when she was most fearful. That love she had known with Ilyas could turn a desert abode into a circus tent for a moment, and the thought of her mother's smile or laughter could still soothe her.

Because she had known love.

Ilyas hadn't.

He had been born to a world without love.

'I don't know how to contact him,' Maggie fretted. 'I don't know if I should try to call or write.'

Flo screwed up her nose at both those ideas but then she brightened. 'His brother's at Dion's tonight.'

'How do you know?'

'Because Prince Hazin gets kicked out of there every Friday. It's the reason they're so popular now!'

Flo knew where all the rich and beautiful gathered!

Dion's was a bar set within a very plush hotel. It had once been a place to gather for pre-theatre drinks. It was old-fashioned but lately had become oddly trendy—a sort of retro, fifties-style bar that now had people lining up to get in.

'You've spoken to him before,' Flo said. 'Why don't you go there tonight and tell Hazin that you need to speak with his brother?'

'Oh, so I just walk in and tap him on the shoulder?' Maggie said dryly. 'I doubt he'll even remember me. And, anyway, I'll never get in.'

Dion's was terribly exclusive and a playground for the seriously rich, but Flo knew one of the doormen and she knew what it took to get in.

'Dress up!' Flo said. 'Wear black and leave your hair down and show some of that fabulous new cleavage. No one will be looking at your stomach!' She waved away the exclusive entry requirements as if they were nothing more than a slight irritation but Maggie remained hesitant and shook her head.

'I can't.'

'Of course you can—I'll come with you.'

'You're working.'

'I can be there by ten, unless I'm in with a delivery.'

'I'll never get in on my own.'

'Then you'll have to wait outside till I get there—I wouldn't leave you mid-second-stage labour.' Flo smiled and gathered her bag. 'I'm an amazing midwife, you don't know what you're missing out on.'

And then she was gone, leaving Maggie with her head spinning.

She had wanted to talk to Flo about the *possibility* of letting Ilyas know.

Now she had an actual chance to.

Tonight.

Maggie showered and as she ran the soap over her stomach she felt the swell of the little life within. If nothing came of tonight, at least she could later say that she'd tried to make contact.

And so she dried off and took for ever trying to sort out her hair. Flo had said to wear it down, but it was too wild for that and too freshly washed to wear up.

In the end, she smoothed it as best she could and settled for down.

It had been for ever since she had bothered with make-up but, given that it was Dion's she was trying to get into, Maggie gave it a good go.

She put on an ivory foundation that made her look as if she should be heading out to haunt houses instead of meeting a prince in a cocktail bar, but a dash of rouge took care of that. She put on a neutral eye shadow but added eyeliner and lashings of mascara.

It was actually fun to dress up.

In fact, it had been too long since she had.

A year of backpacking had put paid to stilettos, and even before that Maggie had never really been one for painting the town red.

She painted her lips red tonight, though.

Flo wouldn't recognise her, Maggie thought, let alone Hazin.

Her one little black dress wasn't really designed for a pregnant woman, but she squeezed herself into it and arranged her rather spectacular cleavage. There wasn't loads but she had started with so little that it was certainly a change. Then Maggie topped the look off with stilettos and teetered to the mirror.

There was something missing…

Maggie wasn't sure what it was because she tried a necklace but that was too much, and she tried a little wrap to cover her very white arms, but that just looked stupid.

And there were no stockings in her drawer.

She would just have to do.

Maggie was reciting her rehearsed lines as she checked her purse.

'Hi, Hazin.' She did her best breezy voice. 'We met a few months ago…'

Or, 'Hi Hazin, it's Maggie, the girl in the green bikini…'

No!

'Hi, Hazin,' she said in a serious voice. 'Could you tell Ilyas that I need to speak with him…?'

All her opening lines were terrible, Maggie knew, and she was consoling herself that she would never get past the doorman to even try them.

She locked up her little room and then headed down the hall and opened the front door… And there he was.

The *something* that was missing.

The very thing that had been missing since the morning they had said goodbye, the man she had been telling her heart to get over, all the while knowing that she never, ever would.

'Maggie.'

Ilyas sounded so formal, yet just a little unsure.

He was wearing a suit and tie—and wearing it terribly well—but it messed with her fantasies, because she saw him at all times in a robe, or naked, or in those black harem pants he had worn.

Yet here he was immaculate in deep navy with a crisp white shirt and tie, and his jaw was clean shaven.

His voice was a touch uncertain, for, far from missing him, Maggie was clearly on her way out.

'You were supposed to answer the door in pyjamas with red eyes and a bucket of ice cream,' Ilyas told her.

'That was last night.' Maggie smiled. 'And how dare you come to my door looking so different from how I remember you?'

'I was supposed to be meeting with my brother.'

Maggie was about to tell him she had intended to do the same when he utterly floored her, for Ilyas said something she'd never thought he would.

'I could not bear to leave things, though, not for even one more night.'

He took a step forward and she held open the door.

They walked down the hall that housed the shared bathroom and kitchen and Maggie had to get her keys out for her room on the left.

As she did so, she wondered how to tell him the news, for he couldn't have noticed, given he hadn't said anything.

Perhaps Flo's suggestion to rely on a mass of red hair and a flash of cleavage had worked a little too well!

Ilyas knew.

The second he had seen her he had known, but he was used to keeping his expression from betraying his thoughts.

'I don't think I made the bed,' she admitted as she fumbled with the door.

'It doesn't matter.'

He walked into the small home she had made and he was so incredibly proud of her for picking herself up and starting over again and again.

And she was very pregnant.

Ilyas needed a moment to centre himself and for the news to take hold.

He was a planner.

But there were times when the world upended even the very best laid plans.

He had left with his country's future planned yet still somewhat uncertain, having jeered to his father that he had no heir.

And then, when his head was swirling, he saw something and he walked over and picked up the glass bottle and held it in his palm. 'The sands of home?' he checked.

'Yes.'

He removed the stopper and peppered his palm with grains and drew on their wisdom.

All would be well.

'Ilyas…' He heard the nervousness in her voice and responded to it with warmth.

'Yes…?'

It took only a moment and when he walked over, his palm went straight to her stomach and his touch embraced them both—mother and child.

His arms were the luxury she had missed, Maggie knew as he pulled her towards him.

When there, her mind did not search for answers, she just let herself be held.

Maggie had been so unsure how to tell him, and had made herself dizzy trying to fathom what his reaction would be. But Ilyas's embrace was just right, and then his tender touch to her stomach told her all would be well.

Maggie did not know what would happen, but if an occasional lover was all she could be, she would take it, because there could be no one else for her than Ilyas.

She breathed in his scent, so familiar to her soul, and each nerve flared in instant recall and with desire.

Oh, she had missed him so much.

Words were not required now, and instead she succumbed to the bliss of his kiss. She did have a fuse, it just required Ilyas to ignite it. And so very easily he did.

He kissed her down onto the unmade bed and when they ached for skin-to-skin contact there simply was no time, for their needs had been left unaddressed for too long.

Ilyas ran a hand between her bare legs as her dress ruched up.

The lipstick she had so carefully applied smeared both their mouths as she held his cheeks in her hands.

Ilyas took delicious care of the rest.

He tore at her knickers and he unzipped.

As she moved to open her legs, it was not fast enough for Ilyas, and his impatient hand was already there, parting them. His breath felt hot on her ear, and then Maggie closed her eyes as he slid in and filled her.

He took his weight off her, but she wrapped her legs around him and dragged him closer. Their lovemaking was intense and frantic and he took her hard and deep. She held his broad shoulders and Maggie ached for his skin to be against hers, but he was fully dressed, the only naked part of him deep inside her.

She was suddenly frantic, her hands patting his suited shoulders as if somehow she might find the flesh beneath.

'Ilyas…' she gasped, for she was trying to hold on, scared that her orgasm might herald the end of a torrid dream for, even now, she could still not quite believe he was there.

Then he gave a low shout and she could no longer hold back as he shot into her and she came hard to him—tight, intimate beats, dragging out each precious drop he delivered.

And they were lovers again, Maggie thought as he pulled out of her. In a moment, she thought, they would get undressed, but for now they were breathless and anything other than holding the other seemed like too much effort.

He pulled her dress down a little and he arranged himself, and then his hand came to her stomach and Maggie felt his curiosity about the changes in her.

And, of course, he had questions.

'When did you find out?' he asked with his hand on her stomach.

'A few weeks after I got back,' Maggie admitted.

'Were you scared?'

She nodded.

'Of me?'

'No. I think I was more scared of our baby being without you,' Maggie said. 'And I was scared what might happen…'

'I hate the thought of you alone and dealing with this.'

'I wasn't alone. I had Flo and Paul…' She closed her eyes because tears were threatening.

'You *can* cry,' he said.

'I don't, though,' Maggie said, and blew out a breath. She told him what she had found out the day before.

'It's a little boy,' Maggie said.

Ilyas let that sink in.

A boy.

He would have a son. He did not need to swear that he would be a better father than his own. There was no doubt in his mind as to that.

And there was no needless questioning as to whether or not he was the father, but there was one thing he needed to know. 'Were you ever going to tell me, Maggie?'

She looked up at him. 'I was on my way to.'

He raised a disbelieving eyebrow.

'I truly was. I'm supposed to be meeting…' Maggie let out a yelp and then she leapt from his arms and off the bed and raced for her purse and phone. 'Oh, I was supposed to be meeting Flo…' She felt terrible at the thought of her standing outside Dion's alone.

'Your friend?' he checked. 'So what happened to telling me?'

'Flo was going to help get me into Dion's. It's a bar— apparently your brother is there tonight…'

The fear of never knowing about his son left him then, for he would have been told tonight.

Perhaps even by Maggie herself!

'I arranged to meet Hazin there tonight too,' Ilyas admitted. 'I need to speak to him and I thought it would be less formal to do so there.'

'You were on your way there too!'

He nodded.

'I would have died if I'd walked in there and seen you!' Maggie smiled in delight at the thought, and then worried as she read through Flo's texts. 'She says she's left my name at the front and to meet her inside…'

Maggie looked at the time and then she looked at Ilyas, who was wearing a lot of her red lipstick on both his face and shirt. She could only hazard a guess how she must look!

'What do I do?'

'Text her and tell her something came up,' Ilyas suggested, and reached over and pulled her back to the bed. 'Tell her you are sorry but Ilyas proposed and you hope she understands…'

'Proposed?'

'Will you marry me, Maggie?'

She had thought a part-time lover might be the best she could hope for.

'Do you have to marry me because I'm pregnant?'

'No.' Ilyas shook his head. 'I could have the palace deal with all that. I want to marry you. Why do you think I'm here?'

'I don't know.'

'Do you really think I came all this way for sex?'

'Maybe,' she admitted, for she wouldn't put it past him. 'You really came here to ask me to marry you?'

'And for sex,' he said, and watched her start to laugh, but then midway it faded. His Maggie was wise, and instantly she saw the impossibility of it happening in the land she had, a few months ago, left.

'Your father would never agree.'

'I don't need him to. I make the decisions now.'

'But he is king.'

'And I have told him that unless there are changes—big ones—I shall take it to the people.'

It was daunting but Ilyas seemed incredibly calm.

'Maggie, I have been planning this for a long time. Many years ago, I knew that change was required. At first I thought I would have to wait until I was king, but, as the years passed, I knew it was not fair to the people. I have been waiting until the time was right to step up. You—' he smiled '—expedited the process.'

'Me?'

'When you told me I should ask the Bedouins, when our thoughts met and were the same, I knew I could wait no longer for change.

'I have something for you.' He reached into his jacket and he handed her a soft black pouch. When she opened it, into her palm fell a huge, rough, uncut stone.

A ruby.

'It is from the red river,' he told her.

'Every night since you left I have been to the *hammam*…' He saw her purse her lips. 'I have been in the cave pool each night, and this morning, when finally I retrieved this, I knew it was time. I took this stone in with me when I challenged my father. Tonight I bring it to you.'

'You could have drowned.'

'But I didn't.'

She looked at the stone in her hand and thought of all he had been through for her.

'I need to return tomorrow to Zayrinia. I want to be certain that things are moving in the right direction before I bring you there.'

'And if they're not?'

'Then together we shall work out what to do.'

'Together?' she checked.

'Now and always.' He nodded. It was a solemn vow indeed, for he understood now the power of love and having another to share his thoughts with. 'There is one problem, though—I have to take the stone. As soon as I inform the palace that I have offered it to you, we shall have to remain apart until our marriage. That is, if you say yes.'

'Oh, yes!' Maggie said.

'I'm going to take care of you both,' Ilyas told her.

It was overwhelming.

Wonderful.

'When is he due?' Ilyas asked.

'Christmas.'

And finally there was a Christmas she was looking forward to when she hadn't for so long.

'One day, when you're ready…' Ilyas said, for he could see that she fought not to cry, 'I will be there to wipe your tears.'

It was such a comfort to know.

But not tonight, for she leant in to kiss him and her fingers worked to undo his tie, for it was a different comfort she required now.

She wanted him naked, and as Ilyas dealt with the remainder of their clothes, she knew he wanted the same.

Tomorrow he would return to the palace and pave the way to bring back his bride.

And he would do whatever it took.

For now, they had this night.

EPILOGUE

'GOOD LUCK!'

Flo's eyes were a little worried as she wished her friend all the best for this most special day.

'Can't I be with her?' Flo asked again.

'I'm sorry,' Kumu said. 'Only family can be with the bride.'

And Maggie didn't have any.

There were many things that were changing in Zayrinia, but this custom was carved in stone and so Flo left to get ready for the ceremony and Maggie was left alone.

Well, she had Kumu and many maidens but, no, it wasn't the same.

Today, on this her wedding day, she missed her mother so much.

Maggie, Flo, Kelly and Paul had arrived in Zayrinia a couple of days ago. But only Maggie had fully understood the sweeping change and the glimpse of more to come when the car had pulled up at the main entrance to the palace.

There had been a formal greeting and she had smiled politely and curtsied for the king and queen.

Ilyas had told her that the king had accepted the

transition as if he himself had thought of it. And that, if anything, his mother seemed relieved.

The queen actually had a small smile for Maggie, and was far politer in her greeting than she had been the first time.

Of course there was no Ilyas.

For two nights there had been formal dinners and stunning days spent in the *hammam* with Flo, but today the pre-wedding celebrations and preparations had ended.

Maggie sat wearing a muslin slip. Her hair had been done and Kumu was attempting to do her make-up, but tears kept slipping out and she knew that today, of all days, it was imperative she did not cry.

She might never stop if she did.

Maggie wanted the wedding over with. She just wanted to be alone with Ilyas, for despite rehearsals she was terrified she might mess it all up.

Ilyas knew she would be feeling scared and alone.

'Hazin is still not here,' an extremely concerned Mahmoud informed him. 'His jet is still in Dubai.'

But Ilyas had more on his mind than his wayward brother today.

'I want you to find out how Maggie is.'

As Mahmoud walked off to follow his instruction, Ilyas called him back.

'Not just a vague enquiry,' he emphasised. 'Ask Kumu. In fact…' He gave Mahmoud more specific instructions.

It had been a very long two weeks.

Ilyas had not been making idle conversation when he had told Maggie that as soon as he asked her to be his wife they would be kept apart.

That time in the bedroom, that very precious night, had been their last real time together.

He had returned on his royal jet to get back to Zayrinia and put plans under way as Maggie had spent a frantic few days sorting out her rapidly changing life.

Now she took a break from the attempts to make up her face and tried to calm down.

Foolishly perhaps, she looked out of a window and saw the streets below, all lined with people awaiting their first glimpse of the married couple and their first sighting of her when they came out onto the balcony.

Maggie ran a hand over her stomach, which seemed so much bigger than when Ilyas had left. She looked down at the waiting people and knew they would soon find out about the pregnancy, and she was nervous what their reaction would be. Maggie didn't want drama and negativity to surround her son before he was even born.

A cheer went up as a car drove towards the palace and Kumu told her that it was a neighbouring country's king and queen arriving.

'Has Prince Hazin made it yet?' Maggie asked, for she had heard he was causing his usual brand of chaos.

'I don't think so,' Kumu said, and rolled her eyes. 'There will be trouble for him if he isn't here soon.' Then she smiled. 'But no trouble for you. All you have to do today is smile.'

'I will,' Maggie said. She wished she could calm her fluttering nerves, and she did her best to hold back the flood of tears that seemed to well from her throat to her eyes.

'Excuse me a moment,' Kumu said.

Maggie nodded and gazed out of the window and willed herself to be calm. She was cross with herself because she was usually so tough, yet today, when she very much needed to be, she was having trouble pulling herself together. 'Maggie,' Kumu called. 'You need to come with me.'

She was led from the dressing area and down a long hallway and then down several steps. Maggie had long ago stopped asking for a running commentary and had decided to somehow just go with the flow. Kumu opened a large wooden door and she entered a small room with a lattice partition.

Perhaps Kumu had decided to bring her away from windows and to somewhere quieter to attempt her make-up again.

Maggie was guided to a gorgeous high-backed chair where she was instructed to sit.

'I'll come back for you soon.'

'Where are you going?' Maggie asked, but Kumu didn't answer and closed the door. Maggie was left alone. The sun streamed in through a window and it was actually nice to be quiet and still for a little while, for the wedding was just an hour away.

Oh, she wanted her mum!

She could not cry, but her eyes were filling with tears and she loudly sniffed them back.

'Maggie.'

She heard her name and, of course, knew his voice, yet she jolted at the sound.

'Ilyas!' Her response was choked. She was suddenly embarrassed that she had sniffed, but he was not so polite as to ignore it!

'Do you need a handkerchief?'

And just like that, she laughed, and she knew that he smiled as he pressed one through the patterned division.

'It's bad luck to see each other...' Maggie said, for she could make out his profile. Their fingers touched as she took the silk from him.

'Which is why I asked for you to be brought here. Not so long ago this would have been our first date.'

His voice was deep and calming and even if she could not see him, she no longer felt so alone.

'Why did you bring me here?'

'Because I guessed that you might be struggling. I know that your friends would have had to leave you and that you would have been on your own.'

'I'll be okay.' She tried to sound like she meant it and to stop her teeth from chattering. 'It will all be over soon.' She tried to buoy herself. 'It's just a formality...'

'Not to me,' Ilyas said. 'And I don't believe you mean that.'

'No.'

Maggie didn't.

Today was the most important day of her life.

'I want you to enjoy today instead of wishing it was over. We become a family today, and I want you relaxed enough to celebrate that.'

It was the nicest thing he could say to her.

'What are you worried about?' he asked.

'All the people,' she admitted. 'What they will think because, as lovely as the gown is, I look pregnant...'

'Do you remember when I said that the people would not be shocked that I have a healthy sexual appetite?'

She laughed again.

'They know that change is taking place and they are excited to see it happening. I hate the balcony,' Ilyas admitted—something he never envisaged he would.

'When I was a child I would always be scolded for not standing straight or for looking around. Today, I *want* to step out there and have the people meet you. And I shall smile and I shall wave, which I don't usually do, and I shall look around to my wife, and they will see that there is love between us. They will adore you because they will see today just how much I love you. They shall be as thrilled about the baby as I am.'

Maggie sat there with her eyes closed, soothed by his words, but the tears were still trickling down.

'You *can* cry,' he told her.

'Not today,' Maggie said. 'My eyes will be all puffy and my face will be red.'

'And I will still love you.'

'I miss her today…' She couldn't finish. The dam had burst, yet when she finally cried, it was not the deluge she had thought it would be. Instead, deep shudders racked her body and it actually hurt in her chest to let go.

And for Ilyas, it hurt to sit and do nothing other than hear her cry.

But then the hurt stopped for both of them; her tears dried and Maggie felt as if a great weight had been lifted from her.

She had cried alone.

Yet not alone, at the same time.

The grief inside her lifted and she knew her mother would be so excited and proud today.

'I know you miss your mother and I cannot make that go away, but you are not alone today. You have friends here who love you and I will be waiting for you too.'

'I know,' Maggie said, and she no longer felt scared.

'I shall see you soon,' Ilyas told her. 'And I love you.'

'I love you too,' Maggie said, and the words came so easily when she had never thought that they would.

It was a smiling Maggie who looked up when Kumu returned.

'Better?' Kumu asked.

'Much.'

The maidens worked their magic and all traces of puffy eyes vanished, and then it was time to put on her silver robe.

It was heavy and intricately beaded and Kumu helped her put on little silver jewelled slippers. Then it was a slow walk down to the oasis inside the palace where the service would take place.

She smiled at Flo and to Paul and Kelly and then walked over to where Ilyas waited.

And because of that time with him, that time he had given her, Maggie was truly able to enjoy this most wonderful day.

Even the fact that Hazin was missing could not dim the joy.

They stood and faced each other. Maggie looked right into those gorgeous hazel eyes and saw the amber in them glimmer with love as his rich, deep voice delivered its vow. 'I pledge, in honesty and sincerity, to be for you a faithful and helpful husband.'

Now it was time to share a small, sweet fruit and both smiled as they took their piece of a fig and remembered their night in the desert.

Oh, there was so much love to come.

Then he placed in her palm her ruby.

It had been cut and polished to perfection, and when she thought of him diving deep into the cave pool to retrieve it, and how much love he had for her, tears came.

Happy ones, though.

And no one minded a bit.

The only blip in proceedings was the extremely late arrival of Hazin.

They had come through the grand entrance, and were climbing the stairs to go out to the balcony when he arrived.

Wearing a suit, no less.

And looking very dishevelled.

Certainly he was in no state to go out onto the balcony.

'Uh-oh!' Flo said.

'That's Hazin,' Maggie explained, and then saw her friend's lips tighten. 'You've already met?' She frowned.

'At Dion's.'

Flo had told her he'd left by the time she'd got there!

But there was no time for chatter; the people were waiting and Hazin was swaying as if he might soon pass out.

'Go and sleep it off,' Ilyas told his brother sternly. 'I will speak with you later.'

Ilyas dealt with it and then he turned and gave a small eye-roll to his bride, who laughed.

It was a smiling Crown Prince Ilyas who stepped out onto the balcony. He looked out and smiled at the waiting people.

Even the king and queen managed a wave and the people cheered even louder.

Then Ilyas turned to his wife and to the utter delight of the people he gave his bride a kiss on the cheek.

'Happy?' he asked.

'So happy.' Maggie smiled, for she was with the man she loved and finally had her family.

Love had, at long last, returned to the palace.

* * * * *

If you enjoyed
CAPTIVE FOR THE SHEIKH'S PLEASURE
by Carol Marinelli,
look out for the next part of her
RUTHLESS ROYAL SHEIKHS duet!

CHRISTMAS BRIDE FOR THE SHEIKH
Available December 2017 in
Mills & Boon Medical Romance!

And, in the meantime, why not explore
these other Carol Marinelli titles?

SICILIAN'S BABY OF SHAME
THEIR ONE-NIGHT BABY
Available now!

MILLS & BOON®

MODERN™

POWER, PASSION AND IRRESISTIBLE TEMPTATION

MILLS & BOON®

EXCLUSIVE EXTRACT

Leonidas Betancur was presumed dead after a plane crash, and he cannot recall the vows he made to his bride Susannah four years ago. But once tracked down, his memories resurface – and he's ready to collect his belated wedding night! Susannah wants Leonidas to reclaim his empire and free her of his legacy. But dangerously attractive Leonidas steals her innocence with a touch... And the consequences of their passion will bind them together for ever!

Read on for a sneak preview of Caitlin Crews' next story
A BABY TO BIND HIS BRIDE
One Night With Consequences

There was a discreet knock on the paneled door and the doctor stepped back into the room.

"Congratulations, *madame*, *monsieur*," the doctor said, nodding at each of them in turn while Susannah's breath caught in her throat. "The test is positive. You are indeed pregnant, as you suspected."

She barely noticed when Leonidas escorted the doctor from the room. He could have been gone for hours. When he returned he shut the door behind him, enclosing them in the salon that had seemed spacious before, and that was when Susannah walked stiffly around the settee to sit on it.

His dark, tawny gaze had changed, she noticed. It had gone molten. He still held himself still, though she could tell the difference in that, too. It was as if an electrical current ran through him now, charging the air all around him even while his mouth remained in an unsmiling line.

And he looked at her as if she was naked. Stripped. Flesh and bone with nothing left to hide.

"Is it so bad, then?" he asked in a mild sort of tone she didn't believe at all.

Susannah's chest was so heavy, and she couldn't tell if it was the crushing weight of misery or something far more dangerous. She held her belly with one hand as if it was already sticking out. As if the baby might start kicking at any second.

"The Betancur family is a cage," she told him, or the parquet floor beneath the area rug that stretched out in front of the fireplace, and it cost her to speak so precisely. So matter-of-factly. "I don't want to live in a cage. There must be options."

"I am not a cage," Leonidas said with quiet certainty. "The Betancur name has drawbacks, it is true, and most of them were at that gala tonight. But it is also not a cage. On the contrary. I own enough of the world that it is for all intents and purposes yours now. Literally."

"I don't want the world." She didn't realize she'd shot to her feet until she was taking a step toward him, very much as if she thought she might take a swing at him next. As if she'd dare. "I don't need you. I don't *want* you. I want to be free."

He took her face in his hands, holding her fast, and this close his eyes were a storm. Ink dark with gold like lightning, and she felt the buzz of it. Everywhere.

"This is as close as you're going to get, little one," he told her, the sound of that same madness in his gaze, his voice.

And then he claimed her mouth with his.

Don't miss
A BABY TO BIND HIS BRIDE
By Caitlin Crews

Available January 2018
www.millsandboon.co.uk

YOU LOVE
ROMANCE?

WE LOVE
ROMANCE!

For exclusive extracts, competitions
and special offers, find us online:

f facebook.com/millsandboon

𝕏 @MillsandBoon

◎ @MillsandBoonUK

Visit millsandboon.co.uk